Mulatto Girl Aggie, 13: Name on the Ledger

LaKesa Cox

Dedicated to Almeda Crossin –
My grandmother, my angel, my heart.
I miss you more and more each day.

Mulatto Girl Aggie, 13: Name on the Ledger

Chapter 1

Ugggghh. I swear school blows me. I feel like it's a complete waste of time. When will I ever, in my adult life, use congruent polygons? I've never seen my mom or dad plot out trapezoids on graph paper while plotting out the x-axis and y-axis. Instead of teaching me how to dilate a figure, Ms. Mitchell needs to teach me how to invest my money since I plan to be super rich when I grow up. See, I'm going to own a coffee shop franchise, just like Starbucks but a hundred times better. We will have the best coffee, pastries and ice cream! ***Cupz and Conez*** – I already have the name figured out. So, the way I see it, I don't need any of this stuff Ms. Mitchell is teaching. But, my mom, dad and grandma all tell me how important an education is, especially for a woman, a *black* woman. Things are going to be so much harder for me, blah blah blah. I don't get it because I'm not going to be like my mom, working for some big company getting all stressed out from taking verbal abuse in a call center every day. Then there's my dad – worked for ten years at the cigarette factory before getting laid off almost a year ago. I won't be like either of them - I'm going to be my own boss.

Seventh grade does nothing to prepare you for the real world, neither does eighth grade or the four years of high school. All they are doing is teaching us information needed to pass some stupid standardized learning test so the school can meet accreditation. I wish I could bypass the rest of middle school and high school to go straight to college. From what I understand, college is where you get trained to go out into the real world. I don't really know this for a fact since neither one of my parents went to college and I don't know anyone in college, but from what I see on TV, college is where my future really begins. However, if I can figure out a way to open my business without going to college then I won't waste my time there either.

Doodling images on the cover of my notebook seem to keep my eyes from drifting off to sleep while listening as Ms. Mitchell goes over her lesson. Her flowered print skirt dances from side to side with each stroke of her dry erase marker. I almost feel like I'm in a cartoon world, with the letters and numbers dissipating and Ms. Mitchell's words running together.

"Ms. Lucas, are you paying attention?" Ms. Mitchell snaps. Calling me by my last name means she has already tried asking me a question but I was off in another place. She peers at me over her glasses.

"Sorry, I didn't hear what you said. Can you repeat the question?"

"With a dilation, does the overall shape stay the same or does it change?"

I'm stumped. I hadn't been paying attention to her lesson and now it's coming back to bite me in the butt. I do eenie, meanie, minie, moe in my head to figure out the answer.

"Change?"

"No, that is not correct. Aggie, how do you expect to pass the test when you are not focusing in class? I literally went over this two minutes ago."

"I think we should be able to opt out of taking that stupid SOL test. As a matter of fact, SOL stands for Stupid Ole Lessons test. None of this stuff is preparing us for our futures, tell the truth Ms. Mitchell." Some of my classmates snicker softly.

"Aggie, don't start with the disruption today. Believe it or not, there are some students in this class who enjoy learning."

"Raise your hand if you think you will ever use Pre-Algebra in your adult life." The only person to raise his hand is the foreign exchange student from Peru seated two rows over from me who can barely understand English.

"Aggie, I'm warning you. You don't want to learn, that's your choice. But you will respect my class and allow the other students to learn. One more outburst and you're going to the office."

"But Ms. Mitchell, I was minding my own business when you called my name." The kids in class snicker louder. I don't know why I get a kick out of getting under Ms. Mitchell's pale skin, but I do.

"Not another word Aggie." I suck my teeth. Technically, she started the whole thing by calling my name. She should've known I wasn't interested in answering any questions. Since class participation is only 10% of my grade, I prefer to take a loss on it. I'm acing everything else anyway. Give me good notes and I can pass practically every test. Ms. Mitchell shakes her head and continues with her lesson. I know I give these teachers a hard time. Shoot, most of the students here give the teachers a hard time. My mom always says they don't pay the teachers enough to deal with teenagers all day, especially middle school-age teens. Technology probably has a lot to do with it I guess. Social media sensationalizes fights, encourages bullying and give students fake personas to hide behind. At one click, you can find a practical joke from another country. One thing about me, I don't like fighting and despise bullying but I enjoy finding Youtube videos on practical jokes. Combine my jokester persona with the gift of speaking my mind and that equals trouble for me sometimes. As a result, most of my teachers have little patience when dealing with me.

I check the oversized clock on the wall, wondering why there's still thirty minutes left for class. I'm eager to get home, go to bed and get up tomorrow morning since it's my thirteenth birthday. My parents promised me I would get either an IPhone, an IPAD mini or the new Air Jordan 7s for my birthday. I'd done my part by getting all A's on my report card so it was time for them to keep their promise. I prefer the IPhone since my Samsung was so old and out of date, however, either one would make me the happiest girl on the planet. Christmas had its own share of disappointment with money being tight and everything so I know they have to redeem themselves. Besides, turning thirteen is a major milestone and my other friends were all coming up with creative ways to celebrate. My best friend Lexi, whose birthday is a week after mine, is having an all-white party at a club her parents rented out for her. Lexi wanted us to have a joint birthday party, but since my dad has been laid off, my parents can't afford it. So my parents promised me one nice gift and maybe next year I'll have a party.

Ms. Mitchell has started handing out copies of notes for us to study to prepare for the SOL tests. When she gets to my desk she leans over and whispers,

"I will be calling your parents this afternoon." Great, that's all I need, a lecture from my parents the day before my birthday. I roll my eyes when I think Ms.

Mitchell isn't looking but she catches me.

"Keep up the attitude." I just shake my head. I feel so misunderstood. Why is Ms. Mitchell calling my parents anyway? She started the whole thing calling me out in class. Normally the teachers left me alone because they never knew what would come out of my mouth. I couldn't help it. I didn't bite my tongue with those teachers. They all know how I feel about school. I was only there because my parents said I had to be and I guess the law says so too. I catch on really quick and don't need a lot of the instruction that most students need. My grandma said I was gifted that way. Instead of going to Malcom X Middle School in the county I should've gone to Victory Magnet School across town for smart kids. I was tested and passed the entrance exam with flying colors. However, I refused to go to school with a bunch of nerds and squares when I can stay at Malcom X Middle with my friends. Plus, I'm one of the most popular students here. I fought my parents on the decision to stay here and they only agreed to it as long as I keep up with honor roll each marking period. Easy as pie. My behavior is another story.

Chapter 2

The school day finally comes to an end and I was almost anxious to go home until I thought about Ms. Mitchell calling my parents. Normally I would get home before my parents so I could check the answering machine and erase the message when a teacher calls. But since my dad has been home during the day, I have no way of getting to those messages first. Nowadays when my teachers call they reach my dad live.

I'm one of the last kids to get off the bus and the only one who gets off the bus at my bus stop. My neighborhood is decent, filled with older, modest one- and two-level homes but way too many old people if you ask me. The reason being is our house used to belong to my maternal grandma before she died. She lived in this house for as long as I can remember and my mom and aunt grew up in this house. Some of the same people who lived in the neighborhood back when my mom was a kid still live in the neighborhood — hence, all the old people. Mom and Dad updated the house a lot, more than Mom really wanted. It was

Dad's idea to renovate the kitchen, get new cabinets, stainless steel appliances, new floors and granite countertops. It was also Dad's idea to get marble, ceramic tile put in both bathrooms and new wall to wall carpet in all of the bedrooms. The biggest renovation was the addition to the back of the house – Dad's man cave, complete with a wet bar, pool table, flat screen TV and top of the line sound system. I overheard my mom fussing about how she wishes we would've just kept the house the way it was had she known Dad would lose his job.

I walk down the worn, concrete sidewalk of my tree-lined street about a block and a half before turning the corner, praying that my dad's pick-up truck is missing from the driveway. Instead, his black pickup is in the driveway in full sight. Maybe he'll take it easy on me since my birthday is tomorrow. The front gate squeaks as I open it. The cracked, concrete walkway leads me to the brick porch which introduces our two-level, colonial style home. The screen door is closed but the entrance door is open and I can see through the screen past the living room to the kitchen where my dad is sitting at the kitchen table talking on the phone. I can tell by his end of the conversation that he's arguing with Mom again. Ever since he lost his job, they seem to argue more and more. I move out of view and try to listen to what today's argument is about. Apparently the car payment for Mom's 2013 Toyota Camry is going to be late again because Dad only had enough money from his unemployment check to pay the past due utilities. Mom has been using her income to pay the mortgage and both car payments but this month Dad agreed to pay her car payment so Mom could use her car payment money to buy me a nice gift. Dad hasn't kept up his end of the bargain – *again*. Why can't my dad just get another job already?

When it appears my dad has disconnected the call with my mom, I go inside. I stand in the landing for a moment, contemplating if I should go upstairs to my room first or go to the kitchen and talk to Dad. I opt for the latter when I realize dad notices me.

The living room still houses some of my grandma's antique furniture – heavy wood tables and a cream sofa and chair both trimmed in brown wood. I always admired the little brown feet at the bottom of the sofa and chairs. What I don't like is the thick plastic covering on the fabric that sticks to my legs whenever I sit on the sofa wearing shorts. There's also an oversized, grandfather clock against the wall that separates the kitchen from the living room. Dad told my mom he didn't think the living room furniture matched the rest of the décor in the house, but mom said her mother's furniture would always stay with her, whether it matched the contemporary leather and wood dining room furniture in the kitchen or not.

I walk through the living room into the kitchen,

trying to gauge Dad's frustration. I wonder if some of his frustration is about me and perhaps a call he received from my school.

"Hi Dad," I try to sound cavalier while dropping my backpack on the table.

"Hi Aggie. So, you want to tell me what happened at school today? Go ahead, have a seat." Oh boy, here it comes. The chair screeches as I pull it from under the table. Sitting right next to Dad might not be a good idea in the event he wants to haul off and slap me for what I might say. Sometimes I don't have control of my mouth.

"Dad, I didn't do anything wrong. I simply told Ms. Mitchell how Pre-Algebra is not going to help me in the future, that's all. She got all sensitive when the kids laughed."

"That's all huh? So you don't think you disrupted class with your little outburst?"

"Oh my God why is everything such a big deal?"

"Well maybe, just maybe, Ms. Mitchell is trying to do her job. She has seven classes of preteens that she is responsible for getting prepared for a test which she has to make sure you all pass. She doesn't need a smart-aleck like you interrupting."

"Interrupting? She interrupted me!"

"Aggie. I don't know how many times I have to tell you this. Being the class clown and seeking unnecessary attention disrupting class is not cool."

"I'm not trying to be cool. I'm just honest."

"Honest and disrespectful while she's just trying to do her job."

"At least she has one." For some reason I thought I said this soft enough so Dad didn't hear me. Boy was I wrong. I study his face for a few seconds. There are more lines in his forehead than usual and I notice a couple of gray hairs have appeared in his sandy-colored hair. His light brown eyes look sad. I feel terrible for my comment.

"You think it's OK to talk to me that way?"

"I didn't mean it like that. I just meant..."

"It doesn't matter how you meant it Aggie. You have absolutely no filter and it's disrespectful. You don't think I'm trying to find a job?"

"I do, it's just...Nevermind. I didn't mean to say what I said. I'm sorry."

"You're not sorry. I blame myself for your behavior. Always telling your mom to go easy on you." A few heavy footsteps can be heard before Grandma Patricia, a.k.a. Nanny, appears. Dad must've picked her up from work. Nanny works a government job and most of the time she catches the bus home because she hates driving but lately Dad has been picking her up from work. She likes to come over and cook us dinner when Mom works overtime. I guess today is overtime day.

"Hmph, I keep telling y'all to stop letting these children get away with saying whatever they want out their mouth. In my day, a child stayed in a child's place. They didn't get into grown folks business."

"I know Mama, I know."

"Hi Nanny."

"Don't you hi Nanny me. How many times have I told you to respect adults, especially your parents and your teachers?"

"I know, I know, I know."

"No, you act like you don't. You really need to learn Aggie. This world can be a cruel place to people like you and me. Do you want the people at that school to label you as a troublemaker? The class clown? Is that what you want?"

"No ma'am."

"First they start out laughing with you then they start out laughing *at* you. You need to straighten up Aggie and take school more serious. My grandmamma wanted to go to school to learn and after the third grade she was forced to quit school and take care of her sisters and brothers. And you know what? Her mama never went to school. You know why? Because in those days, black folks were told they were only good for working the fields even after slavery had been declared illegal. So you need to think about your great, great, grandmamma whenever you decide to take school for granted."

"Yes ma'am."

Nanny fussed a bit to herself I guess about my behavior, who knows. She never completely ended an argument the way most people did. I think it was an old people thing. She turns her back to me and Dad so she could pull pots and pans from the cabinets to start dinner. Dad is looking at me, probably wondering if I heard anything Nanny said.

"What?"

"I know you're disappointed in me for not working right now. I'm not setting a good example as the man of the house." Nanny turns and gives Dad the side eye before pulling some items from the stainless steel refrigerator.

"What Ma?" Nanny just turns away, shaking her head. She's still mumbling something under her breath about children staying in their place. Personally, I want the entire conversation to be over with so I can go to my room. I knew that call from Ms. Mitchell was going to stir up trouble.

□

Dinnertime goes off without a hitch and I was glad I was able to eat Nanny's southern fried chicken and homemade mashed potatoes in peace. Lying in bed, I'd already showered, ironed my clothes for school and was texting with my best friend Lexi when I hear my mom's car pull into the driveway. It was close to eleven o'clock which means Mom had worked fourteen hours today. Nanny was gone home and Dad was in my parents' bedroom. Technically I'm supposed to be asleep but as long as I was in bed by eleven my parents didn't really put up a fuss.

I hear Mom's footsteps get closer to my bedroom door before my door opens. I close my eyes, pretending to be asleep.

"Stop faking Aggie, I know you're awake." I try to fight the small grin because I know Mom is going to come over and tickle me like she does every night when she works overtime. She always made a point of coming in to talk to me, no matter how late she had to work. As expected, she tickles my side causing me to scream out in laughter.

"I knew you weren't asleep. How was your day?" Mom's eyes are tired and I think all she wants to do is go in her bedroom and crash instead of hearing about my day. It's obvious Dad didn't mention the call from Ms. Mitchell because Mom would not be smiling.

"It was OK. How was your day?"

"It was work. You excited about your birthday tomorrow?"

"Yep. Officially a teenager. Does that mean I get to stay up past eleven on school nights?"

"To do what Aggie?"

"I don't know, just stay up I guess."

"Give me a valid reason why you need to be up past eleven on a school night. If you have valid points, then I might consider it. Otherwise, you know the drill."

"Yeah, yeah, I know." Mom's smile turns into a thin line which means she's about to get serious.

"What is it Mom?" She's about to tell me something, but hesitates.

"You know what, it can wait. Get you some rest and we'll give you your gifts in the morning, OK?"

"OK. Goodnight." Mom pinches my cheek, something she does every night, which I hate because it makes me feel like a baby.

"Mom!" She snickers and exits the room. I wonder why she's so sad. I listen as she makes her way down the hallway pass the walls full of family portraits to her bedroom. When her bedroom door closes, I jump up and open my bedroom door slowly. Most of the time the arguments are muffled so I can never tell what they are arguing about but sometimes they get so heated where I can understand everything they're saying. It doesn't take long for the arguing to start. Mom is saying something about Dad not being a real man and that she's tired of being the woman and the man of the house. Dad says he's trying. Mom says not hard enough. To make matters worse, it sounds like he messed up my birthday. Back and forth they go, Mom blaming Dad and Dad apologizing. Sounds like Mom has had enough. She's tired of working overtime, tired of carrying the load, just tired. Then she tells my dad something she's never said to him before – she told him she wants a divorce. The word stings my ears just hearing it. Sure things have been rough between them lately but never in a million years did I think they were headed to divorce court.

When I hear the knob on my parents' bedroom door I close my door quickly. I hear their bedroom door slam and someone stomps down the stairs and out the front door. When I hear the engine roaring from the Ford F150 truck, I realize it's my dad.

Chapter 3

May 6, 2016 – Happy Birthday to me! It's official, I'm a teenager now. I sit up in bed, grab my cell phone from the nightstand and realize my alarm isn't set to go off for another fifteen minutes. However, I'm more anxious to find out what my parents got me for my birthday. Well, more like my mom since my dad is broke. I wonder if my dad came back home last night. I scramble out of bed and peek out the window. His truck is parked in its normal space, right next to Mom's car. Whew, what a relief. Maybe they worked things out when he came home and divorce is no longer an option. Mom was probably just tired and frustrated when she said she wanted a divorce; I'm sure she didn't mean it.

Looking around at the pink butterfly motif all over my bedroom, I realize it's time to upgrade my bedroom to teen status. A teenager wouldn't be caught dead with such a kiddie room. I wonder if my mom would be willing to upgrade my bed from a twin size to a double?

I slip my feet into my fuzzy slippers and cover up

with my robe before heading to my parents' bedroom. It was almost like Christmas morning for me, instead I would be the only one opening presents. I knock on the door and my dad answers.

"Come in."

Dad is sitting on the edge of the bed facing the door, clad in pajama pants and a white undershirt. Mom is sitting on her side of the bed with her back to both of us. It's as if she's been crying and trying to wipe her face before letting me see her.

"Happy birthday Aggie bear," my mom says before getting up from the bed. She pulls a birthday gift bag from the floor beside her and a smile instantly covers my face. The closer Mom gets to me I notice her eyes are red and puffy. She's been crying. As much as I wanted to know why, I already had an idea and honestly, I didn't want it to ruin my birthday. Mom hands me the gift bag but then pulls back abruptly. She looks at Dad, who's looking at the floor.

"Tony, do you have something to say to Aggie?"

"Oh, I'm sorry. Happy birthday Aggie."

"I'm not talking about that." Dad gives Mom a puzzled look. Mom holds up the gift bag, tighten her lips and her eyes get wide.

"Oh ummm Aggie, come sit down before you open your gift. I need to tell you something." Slowly I creep toward Dad, not looking forward to what he has to say. I sit in the spot he's patting with his hand.

"Your mom worked very hard to get you the gift you really wanted. Unfortunately, she had to take it back to get the money and it's my fault. I know this isn't the gift you wanted and I'm sorry we did this to you again. Christmas we promised you we'd get you what you wanted but I messed up and because I messed up you have to suffer." Dad looks at Mom giving her the green light to hand me the present. I pull out the tissue paper until I reach a box. The box is too big to be an IPhone and too small to be an IPAD. When I pull the box from the bag, I notice it's a tablet - an off-brand, cheap tablet with one of those foreign names that's hard to pronounce. One of those tablets that usually cost $49 at Walmart with the crappy visual display and slow moving apps. Frankly, I can do more on my old Samsung phone than this Lipeo tablet. Tears well up in my eyes.

"I know it's not what you wanted Aggie, but we just don't have it right now. Our priority is to keep a roof over your head, food on the table and clothes on your back. Bills have to be paid to keep us off the street and that's most important. It's not fair to you but I promise I'll make it up to you."

"It's not your fault Mom. I know you're trying to do everything by yourself."

"Aggie, if you want to blame someone, blame me," says Dad.

"I do blame you! It's your fault! Why can't you just

get another job? Work at McDonalds, the mall, anywhere just do something! It's not fair to Mom!"

"Aggie, you don't understand and you need to slow your roll for a minute. I'm your father, I'm an adult and I don't owe you any explanations."

"You screwed up my birthday!"

"Aggie! Watch your mouth!"

"But you did!"

"You going to let her disrespect me like this Cassandra? I'm still the man of this house."

"No you're not! Mom is! She's the man and the woman of the house right now. It's so unfair. I didn't get what I wanted for Christmas and you promised me I would get what I wanted for my birthday. You guys promised me!"

"Aggie, sweetie, I promise, I will get you exactly what you want, it's just going to take me a minute to get it," says Mom.

"But my birthday is today." The tears are flowing now.

"I don't care when your birthday is, it does not give you the right to talk to me any kind of way. I am your father. My job is to protect you and take care of you just like your mom. All I demand in return is respect."

"But you promised." I'm crying a full out ugly cry now.

"I have to go before I miss the bus. Thanks for trying Mom." I put the Lipeo tablet back in the gift bag and hand it to my mom. She may as well take it back and get her $49.

"Aggie! Come back here! Aggie!" Dad yells.

"Tony just let her go. She's upset." Mom's voice trails off behind me as I put as much space between me and them as possible. Why do I have to suffer because they can't stay on top of their parent duties? What are my friends going to think when I tell them my parents gave me a Lipeo tablet? They'll think I'm the biggest joke in town. Compared to Lexi's big birthday bash at a nightclub and Marley's Spa style sleepover at the Residence Inn hotel, my birthday is trash.

I go straight to the bathroom, lock myself inside and finish my cry. 'Get straight A's and we will get you whatever you want, we promise'. I guess it's OK for parents to break promises to their kids even though they preach all the time about keeping your word. 'Always do what you say you're going to do. Do what you say and say what you mean'. Blah, blah, blah. After sitting on the toilet crying my eyes out, I suck it up so I can get ready for school. I need to get myself together otherwise people on the bus will ask me over and over again what's wrong and I don't feel like answering.

Checking my reflection in the mirror, I see my father looking back at me. We are practically twins with light brown eyes, bronze skin and sandy colored, wavy hair only right now I'm sporting shoulder-length box braids and my eyes are puffy from crying. My mom says we are triplets – me, Dad and Nanny since we all three look just alike. There's not a trace of Mom anywhere. New growth was starting to peek through my two-month-old braids like weeds did in cracks of the concrete. I brush my edges down with some gel and decide to put the braids up in a nice bun on top of my head. At least with the bun no one could really detect how much I desperately need my hair redone. Luckily, since my parents can't afford to send me to the African hair braid shop like my friends, Lexi's big sister has talent and does my hair for free. She's really good at it too. I think I'll plan to sleep over at Lexi's this weekend so her sister can redo the front of my braids, give them a fresh look. That way I can get a couple more weeks of wear out of them.

I brush my teeth and wash my face before heading back to my room. Mom and Dad are in deep conversation but at least they're not yelling.

My birthday outfit, which isn't new but one of my favorite hand me downs from my cousin Tia, is hanging on my closet door: True Religion jeans and a real Polo shirt (not a fake one from the flea market). I cleaned my Air Jordans from last year to make them look almost new. I put on my clothes, noticing an envelope on my bed. When I pull the card from the envelope, I open it immediately to reveal a crisp $50 bill. Nanny signed the card in her chicken scratch handwriting. She always gave me cash for my birthday.

At least I could be happy with her gift. The big bunny is hugging the little bunny on the front of the card almost the same way Nanny hugs me. *'To A Wonderful Granddaughter'*. Nanny's card makes me smile. I sit Nanny's card on my dresser after reading the sweet Hallmark message on the inside. I check the time on my cellphone, put on my jean jacket and grab my backpack. Heading down the hallway, I glance at all of my school pictures, from kindergarten through sixth grade, several family portraits and a picture of Nanny in her early years hanging on the wall. There's also an old photo of my mother's mother on a cherry wood stand situated in the corner right before the top of the stairs. I try sneaking down the stairs without my parents hearing to avoid talking to either of them before leaving for school. I don't want the tears to start flowing again. Nanny's card had me in a better mood. Before I can make it to the first step, the creaky floorboards give me away.

"Aggie, come here." Ugh.

"I have to hurry up before I miss my bus."

"I can take you to school if you miss the bus. Come here for a minute." I stomp my way to my parent's bedroom. Dad was going to ruin my mood again, I just know it. I poke my head in the doorway. Mom is in the shower and Dad is sitting on the bed, facing the door.

"Yes?"

"You owe me an apology. I apologized to you for

ruining your birthday and I take full responsibility for messing things up. But you owe me Aggie. I love you more than anything in this world and I would never do anything intentionally to hurt you. You hurt me today, the way you treated me. I'm your father, the only man in this world who would give his life for you. Don't you realize that?" I hunch my shoulders.

"You don't think I would give my life for you?"

"I guess so."

"I know so. Don't you ever disrespect me again. I did you a favor by not telling your mother about the teacher calling me yesterday. Oh you forgot about that huh? You need to understand if there is anything I can do humanly possible to make you happy, I would do it. I feel horrible about not giving you what you wanted and I know this past year hasn't been fun for you. But think about how things used to be when I was working. We ate out every week, I got you everything you asked for didn't I?"

"Yeah."

"Well guess what, things are different now, but only temporary. I'll be back on my feet soon and make it up to you, but in the meantime, you will respect me, do you understand?"

"Yeah."

"Good."

"Are you and Mom getting a divorce?" Dad's eyes get as large as golf balls.

"Why do you ask?"

"I heard you guys arguing last night."

"Look, me and your mom have some things to work out. You just concentrate on staying out of trouble. I don't want any calls today, you understand?" I nod my head, checking the clock on my cell phone. I have eight minutes to make it to the bus stop.

"You want me to drive you to the bus stop?"

"I'll walk, I still have time."

"I love you Aggie bear."

"Love you too."

I manage to make it to the bus stop with a couple of minutes to spare. The light breeze plus the brisk walk I had to do to make it to the bus stop in time have caused my eyes to water. Then again, maybe those were really tears.

Chapter 4

I wait at my locker for Lexi so we can walk to homeroom together – our daily ritual. Today was our odd schedule day so we have two classes together plus homeroom. If my parents hadn't pissed me off so bad, I would've brought my clothes to school and caught the bus home with Lexi. Oh well, we will work it out after school.

I get my Science and History books and put them in my backpack. Lexi, clad in the brand new Air Jordan 7s, is walking hand in hand with her boyfriend Tre'. They make the cutest couple – Lexi with her pretty chocolate skin and long black hair and Tre' with his hazel eyes and copper colored skin. Lexi is part Indian, I mean real Indian by way of her grandfather. He takes her to Pow-Wows and everything. She reminds me of a real live Pocohantas. At first girls used to bully her about her complexion. I think it was because so many guys liked her because of how pretty she is and also the fact she will never have to wear a weave in her life. Her hair can give every Peruvian bundle a run for the money.

Lexi spots me and runs over, leaving Tre' in the dust. We hug when she reaches me.

"Happy birthday BFF!" she squeals. Tre' gives me a head nod which is the equivalent of hello.

"Thank you Lexi. Hey Tre'."

"So what did you get?"

"I don't want to talk about it right now. Can you just ask your mom if I can stay over this weekend?" She turns her head to the side, wondering what's wrong.

"I didn't get what I wanted OK? Just leave it at that."

"I'm sorry Aggie. Hey, at least I got you a little something." Lexi unzips her backpack and pulls out a small, pink, fur gift box.

"What is it?"

"Open it! Hurry up before the bell rings." Inside the box is the most beautiful, sterling silver charm bracelet with a half heart, best friend charm.

"Oh my God, this is so cute!" Lexi dangles her arm in my face, revealing her bracelet with the other half of the heart. I hug her really tight.

"Thank you Lexi. I love it!"

"Nothing but the best for my bestie!" The bell rings and we head to class arm in arm with Tre' trailing behind. Giddy and laughing, we almost knock our homeroom teacher Mr. Waters over when we enter the classroom.

"Young ladies, watch where you're going," he says sternly. We ignore him while heading to our desks. Lexi and I take our normal seats, side by side, in the front of the class while Tre' takes a seat in the back with his friends. Mr. Waters, who is also my History teacher, decided to move our seats to the front because we're too talkative in his class, that's what he says anyway. I'm not sure why he thought moving us to the front of the class would make a difference.

The rest of the students fill the classroom as the late bell rings. Mr. Waters enters the classroom, closing the door behind him. The class is noisy so Mr. Waters goes to the front of the class to get order.

"Quiet down class." Standing in the front of the class, Mr. Waters counts the students quietly to himself before looking over the attendance sheet in his hand.

"Has anyone seen Stacey Martinez this morning?" No one responds. When Mr. Waters bends over to grab a pen from his desk, the bulge from his wallet in his back pocket looks as if his pocket could explode at any time. It's so odd looking, almost as if he is carrying a small brick in his pocket.

"Maybe she's in your wallet. It looks like you have a person in there," I say. The class erupts in laughter because they are all probably thinking the same thing. The size of that wallet is atrocious. Mr. Waters turns to me and his face is beet red. He smooths his thinning hair to the side, careful to cover the bald spot he's been avoiding for years.

"Ms. Lucas, I'm not going to stand for your outbursts today."

"Maybe you should sit down then." More laughter.

"Aggie, one more word and I'm sending you to detention, I mean it."

"Come on Mr. Waters. I'm just playing with you. It's my birthday today. Can't I have a little fun on my birthday?"

"You have your fun at home. School is for learning speaking of which, have you completed your History assignment for my class?"

"I turned it in already."

"Hmph. Class, I'm sure you all have some homework you can be doing right now. I expect you to use this time wisely before first period begins." No one really pays Mr. Waters any attention. Small pockets of conversations start throughout the room. No one ever did any work in homeroom. I chat a while with Lexi, avoiding the whole what-did-your-parents-get-you-for-your-birthday conversation. Mr. Waters approaches my desk and hands me a piece of paper.

"Since you seem to finish your work before everyone else, I think you need something a little more challenging." I look at the paper then look at Mr. Waters up and down.

"You need to challenge your pants to have a conversation with your ankles since they are so far apart from each other." The class didn't give me the reaction I expected. There were more gasps than snickers which meant I probably crossed the line. I look up at Mr. Waters. His lips are pursed tight and his eyes are shooting invisible darts at me.

"Get your stuff and go to detention, right now."

"I'm sorry Mr. Waters I was just joking."

"I don't want to hear it Aggie. Detention, NOW!" He yells so loud his coffee breath hits me in the face. He points his wiry finger at the door. Several 'Oooohs' are floating around the room. Nanny's words are ringing in my ears *First they start out laughing with you, then they start out laughing at you*'. Now I know what she meant.

Mr. Waters scribbles something on a detention slip and hands it to me. I avoid eye contact with the rest of the students, concentrating on the door. It felt like I had to walk a mile just to reach the door. As I shut the door behind me, I can hear Mr. Waters call down to the detention hall to let them know I was on the way. There was no need to try and skip class since they already knew I was coming.

I pass several lockers, first the blue ones, then the orange, before turning the corner toward the administrative offices and detention hall. The library has a few students walking around inside, looking for books. I take in the student art on the walls, self-portraits all done by eighth graders, an annual tradition at the school. A few more feet down the hallway and I reach a gray door with an obscured, glass panel emblazoned with the word 'Detention'. When I open the door, I'm met with two sets of eyes: Mr. Rainer, the detention hall monitor, and a dreadlocked kid from my P.E. class. Mr. Rainer is sitting behind his desk at the front of the small, cramped room.

"Have a seat Ms. Lucas. I understand from Mr. Waters you have some History work to do so you need to get it done while you're in here." I pull my papers and textbook from my backpack and put them on my desk. With all of my clowning around, I'd never been to detention before. The room was gloomy with jail house paint on the walls, no windows, no art, no life.

"Mr. Turner, don't you have some work you should be doing?"

"Ion have nuthin' to do," says the dreadlock kid.

"I'm pretty sure your teacher sent you in here with some work."

"Mane, look, Ion have no work. She put me out the class and sent me here, that's all."

"Well, I expect complete silence while in here. If you don't have any work to do, put your head down on your desk but absolutely no talking or the next step is to the principal. You got it?" I nod my head.

"Mane a'ight," says dreadlock kid.

"My name is Mr. Rainer not Mane," Mr. Rainer says sternly. He reminds me of a drill sergeant with his short, buzz cut and broad shoulders. I can even see muscles through his shirt. I'd bet money that Mr. Rainer was military, probably Marines.

I search the bottom of my backpack for an ink pen. The paper Mr. Waters handed to me was titled 'The Pre-Civil War Era'. Fifty multiple choice questions. My favorite. This should be a breeze. I glance at dreadlock kid who's appearing to dose off to sleep. The secondhand on the wall clock serves as background noise. I want to ask if I can listen to music from my phone with my earphones, but seeing as though we are in detention which is more likened to prison, I doubt if he will allow any special privileges. Instead, I hum softly to myself, flipping through the pages in my History book.

"Be quiet please," Mr. Rainer snaps. Heavy sigh. This is going to be the longest forty minutes of my life.

Chapter 5

"Aggie. Aggie. Aggie wake up." Mom is whispering in my ear but shaking me as if my life is dependent on it. I blink the sleep from eyes, allowing them to focus. Mom's face is so close to mine, our noses are touching.

"What's wrong Mom?" I ask, pulling away from her but when I pull away my hands sweep across dirt. Why am I asleep on the ground? And what happened to Mom's hair? She was wearing a roller set yesterday, but now her hair is packed tightly to her head with a bandana like scarf covering most of it. As a matter of fact, what happened to my mom? She's dressed like a homeless person, those who sleep under the James River bridge tunnel at night and beg for change on Belvidere Street during the day.

"Aggie, we gotta go back now or Massuh is gonna whip us both. Why is you out here by yo'self chile? You wasn't trying to run away was you?"

"Mom, why are you talking like that? And what happened to your clothes? And where are we?" Scanning my immediate surroundings, from where I'm sitting, there is a lot of tall grass and dirt surrounding me in a field as big as a baseball field. Trees line the edge of the field and in the distance I see a big house. A cluster of trees separate one side of the big house from several small, log cabin style houses, which remind me of the green Monopoly game pieces. On the opposite side of the big house there is a huge red barn.

"Why you out here? You know better. Now come on before someone sees." Mom helps me up from the ground then I notice my clothes and the fact I'm not wearing any shoes.

"What happened to my clothes? And where are my shoes? Mom, where are we?" I thought Mom's outfit was hideous but the tethered piece of cloth which was supposed to be a dress on me was worse.

"Shoes? Stop your foolishness now. We gotta go." I wipe my hand on the front of my dress. The dirt blended in with the rest of the filth I was wearing. Mom is pulling at me, ducking through the tall grass so we can go undetected. Then it hit me. I was in a dream. All those History questions about the Pre-Civil War Era were doing a dance inside my unconscious mind. I guess I may as well go along with Mom so I start ducking and dodging too. The tall grass is slapping me against my face and arms and my feet felt gross. I never liked walking barefoot.

"Mom, wait a minute, you're going too fast." Mom yanks me in front of her and puts her index finger up to her lips. We can hear someone walking through the grass. Heaping sections of grass move from side to side like it's doing a dance and out of nowhere a man appears. Mom gasps really loud, caught off guard from his presence. The man's face has a full beard and his hair is long and straggly. He looks very familiar to me.

"What you doing out hea nigger gal? You know you not 'spose to be in this part of the field now don't chu?" Did he just call my mom the 'n' word?

"I'm sorry Massuh Raina sir. Aggie here, she fell down and bumped her head real bad. She just come to. I think she went off looking for twigs in the woods to make a nice mat. You know it's her birthday today?"

"I don't care if it's President James Madison's birthday today, you have no business out here. Now you and yo gal get up there to the plantation before I'm forced to pull out my whip. Get now!"

"Yes Massuh. Come Aggie come!" Mom is pulling me so hard and fast I feel like I'm stuck to the side of a train. I'm still in shock that man called Mom the 'n' word though. Then it dawns on me. That man was Mr. Rainer, from detention hall. What kind of dream am I having?

After being brutally attacked by tall slithers of grass, we finally make it to an area where the grass is short. I look back to see if Mr. Rainer is still following behind us but I don't see him. There is no way he could keep up with us as fast as Mom is running. We both catch our breath as I take in my surroundings. We are in the area where the log cabins are. It almost reminds me of being in the woods at Camp Leguna the way the tiny cabins are clustered together. These cabins are much smaller though and the slots representing windows have no glass. Instead, there are some planks of wood which act as a weather barrier which swing in and out to cover the openings. From what I read in my History book, I'm beginning to realize we are on a slave plantation. Me and Mom must be slaves.

At first we are the only people in the slave quarters, but all of a sudden, other slaves begin to appear.

"Aggie, please don't do that again."

"What did I do Mom?

"You run off in the woods. Certain parts of the woods off limit to slaves you know that."

"Mom, this is a dream, so all of this is not real. We live in the year 2016 and guess what, we have a black president." Mom puts the back of her hand to my forehead.

"You ill chile? This here is 1816. James Madison is the president. You talkin' crazy. You bet not let Massuh hear you talkin' like this. A dream huh! I wish this was a dream and I was up north, living free. We slaves Aggie. Livin' on Waters Plantation in Goochland, Virginia."

"Waters Plantation? Oh my God! Mr. Waters sent me to detention today. He started this mess."

"Oh Aggie you gone get us killed! You have no right to call Massuh Waters Mister. He is Massuh to us. What has happened to you? Ever since your birthday come, you actin' crazy. Promise me, please, you will keep your mouth shut when overseer Raina comes. He's a bad man. You don't wanna get him upset again. He does terrible things to lil' girls Aggie. I just want you to stay out his way you hear?" The fear in her eyes tells me Mom is serious and scared. This whole dream is scaring me because for one, it feels too real. Dreams are supposed to play out like a movie, I shouldn't be feeling anything but I am and it's weird - from the dirt and rocks under my feet to the grass slapping me in my face and arms. I scan the plantation again, watching as a young boy sits in the dirt playing with rocks. Women are walking around like robots, carrying heavy buckets or baskets, all dressed in dirty rags, hair covered with the same type of scarf that Mom is wearing. It's eerily quiet with the exception of light humming sounds coming from the trees.

"It's going to be alright Mom. I won't get us into any trouble. I'll follow your lead. Hopefully this dream will be over soon and I won't be on this plantation much longer." What sounds like thunder roaring in the distance turns out to be a couple of horses heading to the slave quarters. Something I hadn't noticed before was the fact there were no men in the slave quarters initially until the men started to filter in, coming from the area where the big red barn is.

"Oh lawd, where is yo' daddy, lawd where is yo' daddy," Mom cries.

"What's happening now?" I ask but Mom ignores me while searching the line of men with despair. I don't really understand what's going on. When the thunder feels like it's directly below my feet, two white men appear on horses. One of them is Mr. Rainer and the other, clad in tight riding pants, boots and a high collared linen shirt, looks a lot like Mr. Waters. It's hard to get a clear shot of his face because of the shadow from his hat. All of the women slaves are looking through the crowd of men for their men folk just like Mom I presume. Mr. Rainer gets off his horse.

"Listen up. Massuh Waters has come down to talk to y'all so everybody gather round now. Come on hurry up Massuh Waters don't have all day," says Mr. Rainer. Mom grabs me by the arm and we join the crowd of slaves forming around the two men. Mom is still trying to look through the male slaves. Dad is nowhere to be found.

"Oscar, where's my husband?" Mom whispers to an older, male slave standing beside her. The slave's skin is dark like chocolate and he's huge like a football player. He looks at Mom and shakes his head.

"Oh God no!" Mom's legs turn to jelly so Oscar has to hold her up. When all of the slaves have gathered, the well-dressed white man gets off his horse. When the sunlight hits his face, I realize it is definitely Mr. Waters, my teacher.

"Gather round now. Some nice gentleman from Charleston offered me a pretty penny for a few healthy black bucks today. They are on the way to South Carolina as we speak. That is all. Go on your way and don't make a fuss about it." Several women have started weeping softly.

"What does that mean?" I ask Mr. Waters.

"Aggie, remember what we said. Hush now," Mom tries to quiet me but I don't understand.

"Mr. Waters, what did you say?" Gasps all around me. Mr. Rainer comes over and gets in my face.

"Gal, you got a death wish don't you? You address Massuh Waters, as Massuh Waters, you understand?"

"Oh, my bad. Master Waters. I just want to find out what you said just now because I don't understand, something about pennies and bucks." The smack across my face is so intense, it knocks me to the ground and it felt real. I've never felt a pain like that before, almost feels like my jaw is broken. My eyes fill with tears. Mom and Oscar are about to help me up but Mr. Rainer won't let them.

"Leave her there," says Mr. Rainer.

"Massuh Raina, she just a child, she don't know no betta," pleads Mom.

"Maybe I need to teach her a lesson what you think?" says Mr. Rainer.

"Please Massuh Raina, don't' hurt my child. Massuh Waters, I do anything you ask, just don't let him hurt my baby please."

"Sandra, you know the rules. I don't take kindly to sass especially for a nigger gal."

"She not right in the head Massuh. She fell and bumped her head today and she been crazy ever since. Her head just not right. Please just give her one mo' chance."

"My daddy is gone kick yo butt when I tell him what you just did to me you white..." Oscar puts his oversized hand over my mouth and scoops me off the ground.

"Boy, did you hear me? I said leave her be!" says Mr. Rainer. He pushes Oscar who's so much bigger than Mr. Rainer Oscar barely loses his footing. Mr. Waters stands over me. For a moment I think he's going to show me some compassion the way he looks at me.

"Rainer, I think this gal needs to learn some respect. Get the whip," Says Mr. Waters.

"No please Massuh. Think of Ms. Nanny. This here Ms. Nanny's grandbaby. It would break her heart you whip her. Please sir!"

"Nanny will understand. Discipline is required to keep you all in line, you know that. If I let one of you get out of hand then what does that say about me?"

"She just crazy Massuh, that's all. Please don't whip her."

"It's settled Sandra. One lash for being disrespectful to me and overseer Rainer. Keep this up and I might have to whip you too. Rainer, get her to the tree."

"No! No! You can't whip me! Stop it!" Mr. Rainer is dragging me through the dirt and grass by my dress. Rocks and grass slide across my butt and thighs like knives. Kicking and screaming doesn't seem to help. All these grown men and women, standing around letting this man drag a kid on the ground and tie her to a tree. And I thought police brutality was bad. This is unbelievable.

As much of a fight I tried to give him, Mr. Rainer got the best of me. So now, here I am, standing with my face buried in an oak tree with my hands tied, back exposed, getting ready to get whipped like an animal. I close my eyes and just say to myself over and over again 'this is just a dream, this is just a dream, this is just a dream' until the leather penetrates my skin.

Chapter 6

The feeling of a million needles stabbing me in my back rouse me from my sleep. I should be happy for getting out of that horrible dream. Then I open my eyes and turn my head to the left and I'm face to face with some short, wooden chair legs and also at eye level I can see a fireplace. The quilt I'm on is directly on the ground, there's no mattress. Feels like maybe some bird feathers or something are in it but I can still feel the bricks from the floor through the quilt. The pain in my back is excruciating. Why am I still in this God-awful dream?

When I try to turn over on my side, the pain in my back intensifies.

"Owwwww! Mom! Dad!"

Two sets of feet come into eye view. Mom kneels down beside me. The other set of feet pulls the stool over so they can sit down. I can't lift my head to see who it is because if I do, it feels like the wound on my back will split open more. I know it's a woman because she's wearing a dress and apron.

"Aggie, don't try to turn over. Lie still."

"Nanny? Nanny is that you?"

"Yes chile, it's me. Yo mama asked me to come see 'bout you. What you go an make Massuh Waters upset fo?"

"Nanny, all I said was I didn't understand because I didn't."

"You never question Massuh. You never question white folk, period. I done told you that plenty of times Aggie."

"I just wanted to know what he said, that's all. I can't believe Mr. Rainer hit me with a whip."

"Massuh Aggie, it's Massuh. Why you don't learn? Is you crazy for real?" Mom says.

"Y'all don't understand. I don't belong here, this place, this time. I'm from another time, 200 years from now where we don't have masters and slaves and sleep on the floor and walk barefoot outside. We have shoes and clothes and cell phones and a nice house and I go to school and we go out to restaurants to eat sometimes. Well we used to until Dad lost his job. Where is my dad anyway?"

"See Nanny. I told you, she talking crazy. Ever since her birthday come, I think she hit her head on a rock and now she not thinkin' right or talkin' right," Mom says to Nanny, ignoring me.

"I'm not crazy. It's the truth! We have a black president in 2016 where I'm from. His name is Barack

Obama. He's been the president for eight years. There's no slavery in 2016, we are all equal." Nanny pats my leg.

"Now, now don't work yourself tight. Sounds like you havin' some mighty fine dreams in that head of yours. That's alright, that's alright, calm down. I need you to keep still while I put this salve on your back. Massuh Waters must felt bad about sending my boy away, he allow Mistress Pippy to give me some salve for Aggie's back," Nanny says.

"He sent my dad away? When is he coming back?"

"Now Aggie, you know what happen when Massuh send someone away," says Nanny.

"No I don't."

"See Nanny, I told you she bumped her head or somethin'. Her mind gone," says Mom.

I can't see either of their faces now on account I'm so close to the floor and Mom has raised up on her knees to get closer to Nanny. I believe they are whispering to each other.

"Well maybe you just done forgot is all. It's OK Aggie. We gone get you well again. If you ever need to know somethin', you ask me or yo mama. Slaves not allowed to question white folk. Now, whenever Massuh send someone away, he sold 'em to another plantation. Yo' daddy gone to another plantation in Charleston, South C'lina. Yeah, I's always thought my family stays together, Massuh assured me that but......"

"Sold my dad! So that means I'll never see him again?"

"Chances better fo' you than me. Thirty-seven years my boy been wit' me. Longer than most. You still young Aggie. Possible you run across him again," says Nanny. Mom is sniffling, softly crying to herself.

"Run across him again? That's insane!" Tears erupt like a waterfall.

"I want to go home. I don't like this dream. I don't like it here," I sob.

"Shhhh, calm now Aggie. It's alright. Me and yo' Nanny are still here. But you have to promise me you'll keep the racket down. You can't go at Massuh no more. I already lost my husband. You cause too many problems for Massuh, he sell you off too. You have to promise not to talk to Massuh only if he talkin' to you first. And don't you dare look him in his eyes. You can't let 'em think you smarter than them," says Mom.

"Yo' mama's right. They think you smarter than them they break you down to nothin'. You know they caught Oscar's girl behind the barn trying to read a book? Lawd have mercy, they almost skinned that po' girl alive."

"So I'm not allowed to read?"

"You tellin' me you know how to read now? Lawd chile you really is crazy. Please don't say that to nobody," says Nanny.

"But I can read. I told you, I don't belong here. I

don't know why I'm here. I thought it was a dream but I woke up and I'm still here. You have to believe me. I'm not a slave. I know both of you think I'm crazy and you're probably looking at each other thinking I'm crazy, but I'm not." I continue to cry an ugly cry, while Mom tries to console me. She can't hug me because of the wound on my back so she caresses my face while Nanny pats my legs.

"It's alright chile, it's alright," says Nanny. Mom dips a wooden ladle in a wooden bucket, pouring me a cup of water into a tin cup. As much as I want to wipe away whatever germs might be floating around in that bucket, I decide not to since my mouth is so dry. Nanny pulls something from her apron pocket that's wrapped in a handkerchief.

"Here eat this. Mistress Pippy let me take a biscuit from the kitchen. You want some molasses on it?" says Nanny. The biscuit looks nothing like the Grand Pillsbury biscuits we eat at home. This one has a funny shape and it doesn't look soft. However, my stomach sends a signal to my brain that I'm hungry so I agree to eat it. I'm not sure about the molasses but I go ahead and let Mom drizzle some on the biscuit. It's so thick, much thicker than honey. Reluctantly, I eat the biscuit. It actually tastes better than it looks. I'd much rather have some of Mom's homemade lasagna or Nanny's southern fried chicken right now. From the looks of this place, I doubt if they even know what lasagna is.

After eating the biscuit, Mom feeds me a spoonful of some sort of tonic. I don't know what it is but it tastes like furniture polish. Not that I know what furniture polish tastes like, but I imagine it would taste like the tonic. My back isn't throbbing as bad as it has been and Nanny applies more of the salve before getting up and heading for the door. I feel like I want to get up and move around but my back won't let me.

"Where you going Nanny?" I ask.

"Almost dusk so I gotta get back to the main house, help Mistress Pippy get ready for bed. Gotta get up early to go to town with Mistress Pippy to find material to make spring curtains for the dining room."

"You coming back tonight?" I ask Nanny.

"No chile. You know I stays in the slave quarters at the main house."

"Why can't we stay with you?" Nanny cocks her head to the side, still not convinced I don't remember their way of life.

"I keeps forgettin' your mind not right. Before your birthday you stayed inside wit' me. You and me, we mulatto just like yo' daddy. Massuh allowed us to work the main house. But yo' mama not mulatto so she stay here wit' the field hands. I think Massuh Waters had it planned all along to send my boy away, that's why he let you come outside wit yo' mama for comfort I reckon. They didn't expect you to act out. You agreed to work the fields wit yo' mama. You don't remember none of this?" I shake my head no. Tears are welling up in my eyes again.

"Hush yo' fussin' now. I gotta go. Stay here, take care of yo' mama. The two of you need to take care each other. At least you got one another. My boy is gone. All both of 'em now. I's see you tomorrow if I can." Nanny lifts the wooden handle and forces the heavy door open, letting a sliver of light in. Mom leaves the door open and watches Nanny walk away. The sky is a mixture of pink and orange hues and I can see the sun setting over the horizon. Mom shuts the door and sits on the stool beside me.

"You still hungry?" I shake my head no.

"I don't know what happened to you Aggie. I want you to be the way you was. If not, Massuh will surely sell you. I can't stand to lose another family member again." Mom starts crying. She lies down beside me on the quilt, trying her best not to touch my back in the process.

Chapter 7

At first I think I'm hearing a car horn blazing outside, but when I open my eyes, I realize I'm still on Waters Plantation. I can't tell if it's nighttime or the next day since it's dark outside. My back doesn't hurt as bad as before, but still very sore. I sit up slowly trying to follow the sound of the horn. Mom jumps up right after me.

"Mornin' Aggie. Time to get up. I guess you 'member that huh?" Mom is wearing a long, shapeless piece of fabric, it appears to be some sort of handmade nightgown. The fabric looks itchy to me. I notice the scarf is missing from her head. Total opposite of what we do at home, where we sleep in our head scarves, not wear them all day. Her hair looks like it hasn't been combed for weeks. I'm used to seeing Mom's hair straightened compliments of a relaxer, but now she has tufts of matted hair covering her head. She's still pretty to me, with her almond-shaped eyes and flawless brown skin. No one would ever think she's my mother since I don't share one physical trait with her. I thought about what Nanny said, calling me mulatto, her and my daddy too. I guess that means we all look alike?

I watch as Mom pulls the nightgown over her head. She's not wearing a bra or panties which shock me. I try not to stare as it's embarrassing seeing my mother naked. Near the fireplace is a silver, large bucket of water. Mom is using a sponge to wash her private areas. I wonder if I'm supposed to use that same water. And what about brushing my teeth? I don't see toothbrushes or toothpaste anywhere. I guess I'll just go all natural, 100% funky.

"Mom, what does mulatto mean?" Mom pauses for a second then continues to scrub her body with the sponge. I'm waiting to see her add some soap but apparently there isn't any.

"Mulatto means you have some white blood in you. How you think yo' skin got so light and you got them light brown eyes?"

"How come I'm mulatto and you're not?"

"You got yo' daddy's bloodline and he got his from Nanny. Nanny daddy some white man who rape her mama on a plantation out in North C'lina where Nanny born. Then Nanny is raped when she first come here. They say Massuh Waters' daddy is your granddaddy but Nanny won't say."

"What? Oh my God!" Mom grabs her tethered dress from yesterday and slips it over her head. Then she puts on a pair of shorts under her dress, except they look too formal for shorts. She hangs her night garment on a hook on the wall and grabs her head scarf.

"Aggie, what's the fuss about now?"

"How are they able to get away with raping women? Making them pregnant? This is insane! You act like what you just said is normal. That's not normal! Men go to jail for rape!"

Mom ties her scarf on her head and turns to me.

"They go to jail for rapin' white women."

"That's not fair!" Mom walks over to me.

"Aggie, this is how it is fo' us. You gotsta learn. We just slaves here. We property to them, is all. Nanny tells me Massuh Waters has a ledger and he keeps count of all his property, including us slaves. We all in that ledger, alls our names."

"Property? How long am I going to be in this dream! When will this end for me?"

By the fireplace is a black pot sitting on a stack of wood. There's no fire burning but Mom reaches in the pot and grabs something that looks kin to bacon. She reaches on the shelf above the fireplace and pulls down a basket filled with cornbread wrapped in a napkin. Mom puts a piece of cornbread and the thick bacon looking stuff on silver plates for us both and sits it on the wooden table. She gets water from that dirty, wooden bucket again.

"Come, we must eat breakfast. I have slight work today in the fields. Today is Sat'day so I won't be out too long. I'll apply the salve fo' you and you stay put while I work. Please Aggie, don't wander off again like you did yesterday. Promise me."

"Why are you going to work so early? What time is it anyway?"

"Horn blows at 4 AM. Eat Aggie." Mom forces her food down in a rush. I look down at my plate. Man I could go for some Eggo Waffles and scrambled eggs right about now.

"4 AM?! What is this?" The cornbread I can identify but that other stuff was a mystery to me.

"It is salt pork. Comes from pigs. Now eat. I don't have much time."

"How long will you be gone?"

"Until the sun is highest. We don't work too long on Sat'days. Tomorrow we rest so I'll ask Nanny can we do somethin' special fo' you. Didn't get to celebrate yo' birthday."

"Why can't I just go and be with Nanny? I'm scared to be here by myself."

"Aggie, I don't have time for yo' foolishness now. You be alright. Nanny has to go with Mistress Pippy to town. You stay 'round here with the other chil'ren. I ask Ms. Louella look after ya' while I go. She stay right across the way if you need anything. She a old woman but she look after alls the chil'ren while we workin'.

She'll be sitting outside come sun up. Promise me, no running in them woods."

"OK Mom."

"Now turn around, let me put this salve on ya' so I can go." Mom applies the salve then kisses me on the forehead.

"Stay put, ya' hear?"

"OK." She pinches my cheek. Tears are welling up in my eyes. I can't ever remember crying as much in my life as I've cried since being on this plantation. I watch her leave out the door. I hurry over and put the heavy wood down securely to lock the door. I pinch myself a couple of times to see if it hurts. Owww! I can't understand this dream. I've never had a dream where I go to sleep, wake up and I'm still in the dream. I walk around the cabin and study the meager items scattered about. There's no separate kitchen, living room, dining room and of course there's no bathroom. Two mismatch chairs sandwich the small wooden table where me and Mom ate. Then there's the wooden stool, a bit shorter than the chairs with a round base. The quilt where I slept is made of multi-colored patches of material sewn together. Under it is another cover but there's no opening and there are feathers inside for cushion. Maybe this is supposed to be the mattress. There's another one on the opposite side of the room to the right of the fireplace. The door is to the left of the fireplace. There's no dresser or any other furniture other than the table and chairs. A big wooden barrel is in the corner, a big black pot and cast iron pan are in front of the fireplace and a few other dishes are neatly stacked on the shelf above the fireplace. There are several hooks on the walls, some have garments hanging, some are empty. There are no curtains, no pictures on the walls, no rugs on the floor – nothing. In my mind, 200 years doesn't sound like a long time ago, but when I look around this cabin, 200 years are several lifetimes. The only saving grace for me is knowing that I'm just dreaming. Aren't I? I'll see my daddy again. But, what if my 2016 life was a dream and this is my real life? I just don't know what to believe anymore. I know what I'll do, especially since it's still dark outside, I'll go back to sleep. Hopefully I'll be home when I wake up.

Chapter 8

'Knoock, knock, knock, knock'. I open my eyes. Sunlight is creeping through the bottom of the door. Why am I still here? The knocking starts again. I realize there's someone knocking on the door. I panic since I don't know who it could be. What if it's Mr. Rainer coming to taunt me. Or maybe Mr. Waters coming to rape me. My breathing becomes shallow at the thoughts. Getting hit with a whip was one thing but having some dirty white man take advantage of me was a completely different story. I can't classify this as a dream anymore, I'm in a nightmare.

'Knock, knock, knock'. My chest hurts and tears are rolling down my cheeks.

"I just want to go home," I cry softly to myself.

"Aggie?" an unfamiliar raspy, female voice calls my name. Relief sweeps over me when I realize it's not Mr. Rainer or Mr. Waters coming to get me. I open the door and there's this little woman, probably my height and I'm 5'2". Her skin is the color of coal and it's so wrinkle she looks like cracked patent leather. She has a walking cane in her hand and she's dressed similar to Mom except her dress doesn't look as dirty. Her hair is covered with a scarf too.

"I'm Miss Louella. Yo' mama asked me to look afta ya. Told me you not well in the head, rememberin' and all. Been daylight fo a while, I's gettin' worried when you didn't come outside. You alright?"

"Yes, I was sleeping."

"How's yo' back? Need anything?"

I rub my back. Feels like a scab is forming over my wound. I must be dreaming for this wound to heal so fast. That brings me some comfort. Maybe I'll be going back to 2016 soon.

"Back feels fine. Will my mom be back soon?"

"Couple more hours I reckon before sun up high. She'll be back by then. You wanna come outside sit a spell? Other chil'ren out playing by the creek. Think they found some blackberries. Some of 'em over by the barn, collecting corn."

"Collecting corn?"

"After the animals get fed, sometimes they leave some behind. Chil'ren go over and pick up scraps to save for later. Massuh don't give out ration of food 'til Sunday so we eats best we can." The thought of eating leftovers from an animal makes me nauseous. The blackberries I can get with since we find them all the time behind Squirrel Park near the playground by the elementary school. But leftover animal corn? No thanks. Those biscuits Nanny got from the main house don't seem so bad now after all. Neither does the salt pork.

I follow behind Ms. Louella, squinting as we get on the stoop so my eyes can adjust to the sunlight. It's amazing to me how they can tell the time of day just by where the sun is. Mom doesn't have a clock and I'm pretty sure nobody around here has a watch. I wonder how they keep track of the day of the week? The month? The year even. As a matter of fact, how did Mom even know it was my birthday yesterday?

Ms. Louella moves slow, like a turtle. I bet she's about a hundred years old. She makes it to her cabin which is directly across from Mom's. I look around and there are several children running around chasing each other, laughing and playing. None of them are wearing shoes and the ground is mostly dirt, not much grass in the area of the slave quarters. How can they be happy under these horrible conditions?

There's another old lady sitting in a chair about two cabins down from where we are. Ms. Louella waves at the old woman before taking a seat in a chair situated right in front of her cabin. I look around for a chair for me. She points to the raggedy steps leading to her front door. The weather outside is mild, not too cold, not too hot, just right. Perfect May weather. I'm assuming it must still be May especially since Mom recognized my birthday. Ms. Louella and I sit for a moment watching the children play in silence. I'm not sure what I can say and can't say to her since Mom and Nanny have me on talking restriction. I'm sure Ms. Louella is going to say I'm crazy in the head too. I decide to break the ice.

"Those your grandchildren?" I ask.

"Great-grandchil'ren. They mama is my grandchild. She working wit yo' mama."

"How many children do you have?"

"Used to have four chil'ren. Two of my boys killed tryin' to escape long ago. My other boy was sent away. My daughter works in the main house. I like to stay close to my grandchil'ren and great-grandchil'ren."

"Your daughter mulatto too?" Louella looks at me like I said a bad word.

"Half African, like me. Not they fault they got the other half." The way Ms. Louella says this, I feel like I offended her or something. I change the subject.

"You come from Africa?"

"Yes. Come to America when I was twenty-years-old."

"How old are you?"

"Guess I'm about eighty now. Don't really know any mo'. When I was younger it was easy to keep up, not so much now I'm older."

"Why did you come here just to be a slave?"

"You think I want to come here? I was kidnapped from my village. Been in America close to sixty years now. Be glad when I leave here so I can be with my people again." This old lady is not making much sense to me. How is she going to leave here? She could barely walk from here to Mom's cabin.

"How?"

"When I die, then I will be free. Yo' mama was right. You not right in the head no' mo'. Ask too many questions." I get the feeling I'm getting on her nerves and probably more than she bargained for looking after me. I wonder if there are any kids around my age that can show me around. Maybe that girl of Oscar's.

"Where is the creek the kids go to pick blackberries?"

"Yo' mama said you stay put."

"But I thought you said I could go pick blackberries with the other kids?"

"Not a good idea. You talk too much, get in trouble." A fly lands on Ms. Louella's face and she swats it away.

"You don't want me to talk to you so I need to go and find something to do until Mom comes back."`

"Stay put chile."

"Can I go and see if Nanny is back then?"

"You don't listen well do you?"

We sit there in silence for what seems like an eternity when two kids who look to be about my age appear from the woods. One is a girl and she has a small basket full of blackberries. The boy has a bowl with what looks like dirty corn kernels. The girl seems to recognize me because she flashes me a smile. From a distance, I swear she could be Lexi the way her two pigtails are swinging from side to side.

"Hi Grandma Lou. Hey Aggie. You feelin' better?"

"Lexi?" I ask. She looks just like my best friend.

"No, Lettie silly. I'm yo' best friend. You don't 'memba me?"

"No, my memory is not back. I can't remember anything anymore." There was no need trying to explain to them how I'm from 2016. May as well fake amnesia until I get out of this God forsaken place.

"You sound funny Aggie, the way you talk," says Lettie.

"Must be from the bump on the head." I notice the blackberries in her basket. Her fingertips are purple. The boy, who happens to look mulatto like me, is cleaning dirt out of his bowl of corn.

"I don't remember your name," I say to him.

"I'm Phillip."

"I guess my memory is all gone. The only people I remember are Mom and Nanny, that's it. You guys have to help me remember stuff. OK?" Lettie and Phillip chuckle to each other, I think they are getting humor from my dialect.

"Can I have some blackberries?" I ask Lettie.

"Sure. Plenty mo' by the creek. Takin' these in the house for mama so I can go back and collect mo'. You wanna go wit' me?" I look at Ms. Louella, pleading with my eyes. How can I be a prisoner and a slave at the same time?

"You's stubborn as a mule chile. I done told you stay put like yo' mama say."

"But Ms. Louella, I'll be with Lettie, she'll make sure I don't venture off in the wrong direction this time. I promise to behave and keep my mouth shut if I see mister I mean Master Rainer. Please?"

"Yeah Grandma Lou, I'll watch Aggie."

"Lettie, I's countin' on you to behave. Phillip, you goin'?"

"I's goin' to clean dis corn."

"OK. Well you two stay togetha', to the creek and back."

"Yes ma'am," I say. I'm just happy to be able to get away from her and around some people my age. I follow behind Lettie, feeling like we are going on an adventure. I'm a bit nervous since I'm out of my comfort zone. None of this is familiar to me and I have no idea where she's taking me. Lettie takes me down a path through woods which apparently aren't off limits like the woods I was forbidden to go to. The slave quarters disappear behind us and a few minutes later I can hear water flowing, like someone left the water running in the sink in the bathroom.

Near the creek, big clusters of blackberry bushes hug each other as if they'd been planted there on purpose.

"Wow, there's a lot of them huh?" Lettie giggles.

What is so funny?

"Aggie, you forgot to bring a bowl. What you gon' put yo' blackberries in?"

Hmmm, Lettie had a point. Well that's great. I guess I'll have to pick as many as I can, rinse them in the creek and wrap them in this filthy dress.

"I'll carry them in my dress like this," I enact my plan to Lettie, pulling up the bottom of my dress.

"I can't believe yo' memory lost. Do you 'memba our secret?"

"No, what's our secret?" Lettie looks around, searching for sounds of movement. Then she reaches down inside the front of her dress, fumbles a bit trying to release the book she has hidden. The book is small, no color cover like the books I read at the library. It's only about 100 pages and the cover looks like cardboard to me.

"The New England Primer," I read the title. Lettie gasps.

"Aggie, how you know that? Yo' memory not all gone."

"You want to know my secret? I can read. Really well." I open the book, read a couple of the infant child prayers and Lettie almost falls to the ground in astonishment.

"How you do that Aggie? I only know a few of the ABCs, but still struggle with words. My paw told me not to read no mo' since I got skinned fo' it."

"Oscar's your daddy?"

"Yes'm he is. But Aggie, I needsta learn how ta read so I's can read what the abolish, ummm abolishman says about freedom." I tilt my head to the side, trying to understand what Lettie is saying.

"Abolishman?"

"Yes, they's come from up north and help the slaves get to freedom. See," Lettie unfolds a piece of paper she has stuffed in the back of her book. The paper talks about some abolitionist from New Jersey who has been helping escaped slaves get to freedom. He is supposed to be back in the south in July so the slave owners want to capture him. There is a reward for his capture and arrest.

"Where did you get this?"

"Saw it on the road. But I hear abolishman been helping slaves get free. I wants freedom so bad Aggie. I can't take it no mo'!" I don't know if I should really tell her this abolitionist has a bounty on his head and this reads more like a reward announcement than some freedom notice. I fold it back up.

"I's been trying to put the letters together and make words like dis book here say. But I can't understand it all."

"It just says he will be here again in July to help more slaves. That's it."

"July? How many suns is that? I needs to be ready to get to him. They say he has a boat and he waits by the riva at night, over by the tobacco farm near Florence Plantation. He send word when he almost hea."

"Great. Well, I hope to be back in 2016 by then."

"Huh?"

"That's my other secret. I don't belong here. I'm from the year 2016. Somehow I ended up here but I'm going back to my life soon."

"Oh boy, you are crazy like Grandma Lou says."

"I'm not crazy. How do you think I can read so well? Trust me, in 200 years, we are all free. We have our own homes, kids our age go to school and we don't have to sneak and read books. The adults work real jobs and life is good." Less than 48 hours ago, getting that Lipeo tablet for my birthday was the worst thing that could happen to me. Now I'm in this nightmare that won't seem to end, explaining how great life is for us in the future. It didn't feel so great being there then, but I sure wish I was there now to appreciate it.

"Future sounds mighty fine to me. I would love to go to school and learn like the white chil'ren. I's not looking forward to working the tobacco fields come harvest time. Dat's why I have to get to the abolishman. Massuh putting me in the fields. Paw says tobacco fields no place for young girl like me."

"Why you not in the fields now?"

"Tobacco not ready yet. Alls they doin' now is getting' the ground ready fo' it. Besides, I just became a woman now so I hasta work harder. I used to work at da' barn wit' da horses and pigs but when I became a woman, time fo' the fields." No matter what period of civilization, every girl knows what becoming a woman really means. How in the world do you manage having a menstrual cycle in these conditions? No way to take a bath or shower? And what on earth do the women use? Just thinking about it makes me cringe. I want to ask Lettie more questions but then I think about Ms. Louella saying I talk too much. Plus I promised Mom I would only ask her questions if I had any. I doubt if Lettie would tell anyone how much I questioned her but a promise is a promise.

"So Aggie, you gon' help me wit' my readin'? We has plenty sunlight today. We can eat blackberries if'n we get hungry."

"I don't know Lettie. What if we get caught? Haven't you gotten whipped already for trying to read?"

"I thought yo' memory bad."

"No, Nanny told me about it. I promised them I would stay out of trouble. If trying to read already got you skinned, why do you want to learn so bad?"

"You say you not from this time, this place right? You from 200 years where you's free. I neva been free befo' but it better than this life right?" The yearning and desperation in her eyes tell me I have to help her. I know how she feels. She wants freedom just as bad as I want to go back to my life of freedom in 2016. I've only had to struggle with wanting freedom for less than 48 hours while she's been struggling her entire life.

We sit a while by the creek, propped against an oak tree eating blackberries and going over ABCs in the book. I take my time explaining how each letter sounds and what happens when you put them together to form words. It amazes me how easy Lettie learns. Every time she gets a word right, her face lights up. *'Believe it or not, there are some students in this class who enjoy learning.'* Ms. Mitchell's words ring in my ear. Lettie would be happy going to school and learning. Tears start to roll down my cheek.

"What's wrong Aggie?"

"I want to go home."

Chapter 9

I don't know how much time I spent at the creek with Lettie teaching her to read, but somehow she was able to look up at the sun and know it was time to get back to the plantation. She tucks her book away in a handmade pouch which hung from a small piece of rope around her neck. It was hidden underneath her dress. We follow the same path we took to get to the creek back to the plantation, stopping for a minute to look out into field.

"See all that field Aggie? You an' me gone be working like mules tendin' to them fields. We gotsta help each other get away from here." On the opposite side of the field, we see men and women slaves walking in a straight line towards the plantation. Mr. Rainer is on his horse, escorting them along the way.

"Come on Aggie. We gotsta beat them home." I follow Lettie as she runs through the field, getting slapped around by grass again.

"Why do we have to get home before them?" I try talking in between sucking in air to keep me from passing out. On top of that, my back is starting to throb.

I thought Mom ran fast, well Lettie belongs in the Olympics.

"Gotsta hide my book or else mama and paw find out I still trying to read. Come Aggie, hurry!" Lettie takes us through a short cut and we end up in the back of the slave quarters near a section where a larger cabin is housed and what looks like a water well. Smoke is coming from the chimney of the larger cabin and it smells like bacon frying. There aren't many children playing in this area, but there are a few dogs sniffing around, probably trying to get a taste of the pork that's cooking.

"Smells good over here," I say. The smell reminds me of Mom frying pork chops. What I wouldn't do for a pork chop right about now.

Lettie checks her surroundings before removing the book from her pouch. There is a rusty tin box hidden amongst some rocks which lead up to an outside cooking pit. Lettie puts the book in the tin box and hides it underneath the rocks. Not too good of a hiding place if you ask me.

'Who lives in the big cabin where the smell is coming from?"

"Remember Phillip? His family. His maw and aunts, they cook food for the slaves. We go there to get food, take it back to our cabins. Since today Sat'day, they all tries to bring whateva food left from the week to cook for Sat'day night. Some folk food be all gone so we all try and make sure everybody eat today. Tomorrow Massuh give us all our food." Immediately I think about Phillip and that dirty corn. Disgusting. As if on queue, Phillip emerges from the cabin, sweaty with no shirt on. For a boy my age, he sure does have muscles. Phillip smiles when he sees us, waving really hard at Lettie.

"I think he likes you," I say.

"I know. My paw said Phillip keep sniffin' round me like a dog in heat. Phillip always talking foolish about us jumpin' the broom."

"Jumping the broom? Wow, I saw a movie called Jumping the Broom before. People really do that huh?"

"Movie? What's that mean?"

"We have something called television where I'm from and we watch television for entertainment. Movies come on television and movies are not real just made up stories with actors and actresses who make the stories seem real when we watch them. Does that make sense?"

Lettie is looking at me like I have three eyes. None of this makes sense to her. Honestly, I'm having a hard time explaining movies and TV to her.

"I know what, you know how in some books they tell a story? Well, television movies are just stories, like stories you read except you get to see them played out on a screen. Does that make sense?" Lettie shakes her head no. I guess it wouldn't make sense to me either. I need to find out when TVs and movies were invented if I ever get back to my life.

"Back to this jumping the broom thing. So is Phillip going to be your husband?"

"Let Phillip say it yes but I plan on marryin' a free man. I ain't marryin' no slave." We walk away from Phillip's cabin toward Mom's and notice Ms. Louella is still sitting in the same spot we left her in. A lot of women and men have started to trickle in from the field. The closer we get to Ms. Louella, I notice her eyes are closed.

"Grandma Lou?" Lettie taps Ms. Louella softly and her eyes open.

"You girls not just getting' back from the creek eh?"

"Yes'm. We fell asleep by the water. We's just being girls Grandma Lou is all."

"Not safe fallin' asleep by yo'self." Ms. Louella stretches her wrinkled arms above her head and lets out a loud yawn.

"Smell cookin'. Times to eat in a while?" she says.

"Yes'm," Lettie responds. Amazing how Lettie laughed at the way I talk. The slave dialect is pretty interesting to listen to. They chop up all of their words.

Ms. Louella stands probably as slow as she walks, propping her weight on her wooden cane and balancing herself. Lettie offers her shoulder as support and Ms. Louella uses Lettie to help her up the raggedy stairs to the entrance of her cabin. I keep a watchful eye out for my mom in the sea of men and women returning from working in the fields. None of them are smiling, instead they all have somber looks on their faces. Almost reminds me of the look Mom has when she comes home after working overtime. Oscar, wiping sweat from his face, is walking towards me and Lettie. Even more sweat glistens on his chiseled, chocolate arms. Not far behind Oscar, I notice Mom. She's walking on the balls of her feet like she's trying to avoid stepping on glass or something and her shoulders are sagging. I guess the fields did a number on her today. I wish my Dad was here for her. Thinking about my Dad makes me sad. I wish I hadn't said the things I said to him when we talked last. Looking around at Oscar and all the rest of the men, I realize they probably work the hardest on the plantation but get the most disrespect from the white people. One minute you're working the fields, the next minute they ship you off to another plantation. No warning, no chance to say goodbye to your family, nothing. And, you can't do anything about it. You can't fight it or contest it you just have to deal with it because they own you. Almost like Daddy's job at the factory. He did ten years for that company and they decided they didn't want him anymore so they fired him. It didn't matter he had a family at home that relied on him, they could care less. He had to adjust to not having a job, while the factory went on about its business.

Oscar hugs Lettie.

"Aggie and Lettie, no trouble today?" Oscar asks.

"No Paw, no trouble at all." Lettie looks at me and winks. She looks over her dad's shoulder.

"Where's Mama?" Oscar looks at Mom like they have a secret.

"Hi Mom."

"Hi Aggie. Come on, let's go inside."

"Paw, where's Mama?"

"She had to go with Massuh Raina."

"Why?"

"Lettie, don't ask me 'bout it OK? Let's go inside and get ready for suppa."

"Why you let him do it? Why Paw?"

"What I's 'spose to do Lettie? I get whip if I speak up or worse I get shot. You know Massuh Raina and how he is."

"Aggie let's go. Let Oscar and Lettie talk." I follow behind Mom back to her cabin. Looking back at Lettie, she's crying at the thought of what Mr. Rainer is doing to her mother. I wonder if my daddy was here would he let Mr. Rainer do that to my mom. Then again, what could he do? I guess the same as Oscar – nothing.

We go inside the cabin and Mom sits in a chair, untying her leather boots. When she pulls off her boots, her feet are swollen, reminding me of the jar of pickled pig feet that sit on the counter at Mo's Convenience Store on Nine Mile Road in the city. Mom didn't like me hanging out around there because it was near the projects, however, my Uncle Richard's girlfriend lives over there and so does my cousin Tia. Tia and I would walk to the convenience store to get Hot Cheetos, bubblegum and Mountain Dew.

"I thought you were going to be done by lunch time?"

"Lunch? Hmph. Chile we lucky to get breakfast and dinner. I swear Aggie, I'll be glad when you get yo' memory back. What did you do today? Stay out of trouble I hope."

"Yes, no trouble to report. I hung out with Lettie down by the creek, picking blackberries." Mom looks at me perplexed.

"Me and Lettie stayed at the creek a while picking blackberries." Now she understands. Hung out is probably the wrong slang to use especially on a plantation.

"How is your back?"

"Better, still a bit sore."

"I'll put more salve on it. Just need to rub my feet a spell." I move the stool over close to Mom so I can help rub her feet.

"Thank you Aggie. Yo' daddy always help rub my feet. I do miss him." Mom is fighting back tears. Never one to be at a loss for words, I couldn't find the right words to say. I'm sad for Mom.

Sounds of yelling outside break up the quiet in the room. Mom and I get up to go to the door to see what all the commotion is about. I move faster than Mom, getting to the door first. 'BOOM'!

"What was that?" I ask.

"Sound like a gunshot. Lawd I hope nobody tried escaping today. Open the door Aggie."

I do as I'm told and see men, women and children start to gather around a person on the ground but I can't see who. Mr. Rainer is on his horse, gun in hand. A loud shriek pierces through the sky, scaring the birds from the trees.

"Lawd what don' happen?" Mom asks.

"I don't know, I can't see." Mom wobbles on her swollen feet to the door and we both try to figure out what's going on.

"Anybody else feel brave enough to go up against my authority? Speak now!" yells Mr. Rainer. Lettie runs to the crowd, yelling for her mother Sylvie, who I recognize is on the ground, on her knees. She is rocking back and forth, screaming at the top of her lungs. Her husband, Oscar, is laid out in front of her, dead from a gunshot wound to the chest, courtesy of Mr. Rainer.

"Mom, it's Oscar!" I yell.

"Oh no, lawd no!" says Mom. I run over to Lettie, who is yelling at Mr. Rainer.

"Why?! Why you have to do this? Why?" Lettie yells.

"Gal, you keep sassin' and you gon' be laid there beside yo' daddy." Sylvie, who is equally as beautiful as Lettie with the same black, wavy hair and smooth skin, puts her head on Oscar's chest. It's clear to me he's gone, based on the big, bloody hole in his chest. The sound of horses galloping in the distance gets closer. Around the bend comes Mr. Waters.

"Rainer, what is going on down here? I just heard a gunshot," Mr. Waters ask.

"That there nigger bucked at me so I had to shoot him."

"Bucked at you for what?"

"All because he was upset about his wench." The scene is not as chaotic as one in my time when someone gets shot, but Lettie is hysterical enough for everyone. Other than Lettie and Sylvie, no one else shows emotion. Mr. Waters looks around, trying to figure out which slave might be willing to provide him with the full story. He can tell by the look on their faces they don't want to be involved. Any involvement puts them in Mr. Rainer's bad graces and everyone tried to stay clear of Mr. Rainer.

"Sylvie, get ova here and tell me what happened to Oscar," says Mr. Waters.

"He killed my paw Massuh Waters. Killed my paw because paw stood up for mama. He's tired of Massuh Raina taking her in the barn, having his way wit' her,"

Lettie yells out before Sylvie has a chance to speak. I go over and stand beside my Mom who has finally made it from her cabin after moving slow.

"Is that true Rainer?"

"Who cares?" says Mr. Rainer.

"I care seeing as though Oscar is my property. I just sold some of my best slaves and you go and kill one of the strongest bucks on my plantation? Have you lost your mind? You do realize you will reimburse me for Oscar's worth?"

Mr. Rainer doesn't appreciate being reprimanded in front of the slaves but everyone knows who calls all the shots. He nods like a child.

"Y'all take care of this for Sylvie and Lettie. Somebody go on and alert undertaker George so he can get the body ready for burial. Get him down the hill before it gets too late. Get on now. Mr. Rainer, meet me back at the house." Mr. Waters take the lead. Mr. Rainer, with fire in his eyes, spits on the ground then follows behind Mr. Waters.

The women huddle around Lettie and Sylvie to comfort them while a group of men collect Oscar's body from the ground. Heading beyond the slave quarters, they carry Oscar's body to a hill which appears to disappear into the woods. A few other men have gathered shovels and other digging tools and follow behind the body.

"What are they going to do Mom?" I whisper.

"Going to the cem'tery, dig a hole to bury Oscar. George is the slave undertaker. He get Oscar body ready for burial. Umph, umph, umph, what Sylvie gone do wit' all those chil'ren without Oscar. Guess they's try to do the funeral tomorrow night. I don't know. Po' Sylvie."

The crowd starts to dissipate. Lettie's younger sisters and brothers are huddled around her, holding on to one another. Sylvie appears to be too weak to walk so two other slave women are helping her to her cabin. I walk over to Lettie.

"I'm so sorry about your daddy Lettie." Lettie wipes the tears from her face. Her siblings all have a look of shock on their faces. None of them are crying, just holding each other tight.

Chapter 10

The melodic sound of crickets provide the soundtrack to an otherwise gloomy and sad evening. Beyond the trees I look for the sun setting, wondering if this is the same sun I've watched so many times before while sitting on my front porch at home with Nanny, Mom and Dad, drinking homemade lemonade. Over and over in my head, as time continues to move, I wonder if those were dreams and this is my reality. I've never had a dream or nightmare last this long. No dream has ever been so real before in my life. Maybe I did hit my head and all these thoughts are a figment of my imagination. This has been my reality all the time, maybe. I just don't know what to think anymore.

Sitting on the wooden steps of Mom's cabin, I use a twig and doodle in the dirt. Left behind in my mouth is the taste of the mystery beans and fatback we ate over an hour ago. It wasn't the best meal, but it was nourishment. I sure wish I had a toothbrush. I wonder if they have simple necessities like toothbrushes in the main house? I spell out my full name in the dirt. Tears roll down my cheeks. Maybe I won't be able to go back to 2016 ever again. If that's the case, I need to start thinking of a way to escape from slavery and at least find freedom. I had a weapon that the majority of the slaves didn't – I can write.

Some of the slaves are sitting outside, fires burning, talking to each other. Mom said Sundays were days of rest so no one had to get up early tomorrow for work. The fires danced across their faces in the darkness. It was hard to make out who was who. I notice Ms. Louella standing in her doorway holding a candle. I wasn't quite sure how or if she was related to Sylvie and Lettie, but I go over anyway to offer my condolences.

"Ms. Louella?"

"Yes Aggie."

"Were you some kin to Oscar?"

"Naw, me an' Oscar no kin. Everybody calls me Grandma Lou but I's not everybody's grandma. I have some grandchil'ren and great grandchil'ren of my own tho'." I kick a rock with my foot.

"Somethin' you need Aggie?"

"I was just wondering if Oscar was related to you, that's all. Came over to say I was sorry for your loss but..."

"Oscar was a good man. He took care of his family and everybody else's family. He did a lot for me, just like he was my kin. Massuh Raina the devil. No reason to kill Oscar that way. Good thing now, Oscar free. Go on home chile." I look over at Mom's cabin. I refuse to refer to that place as my home.

"Think I'll go and check on Lettie. See you later Miss, I mean Grandma Lou." I couldn't see Ms. Louella's entire face, but I noticed a small smile.

"G'night Aggie." The candle seems to do a dance as it moves further inside the cabin. There are mostly adults outside now, no small children in sight. That's one thing that hasn't changed, generation after generation – when it's time for the children to go to bed, they go to bed. I chuckle thinking about asking my Mom if I can stay up past eleven on school nights. What was it she wanted? Oh yeah, a valid reason someone my age needed to be up past eleven. I miss my bed, even my kiddie butterfly motif in my room.

Passing several cabins, I finally reach Lettie's. The door is closed and I can't see any candle light flickering inside. In fact, I have no idea what time it is. Maybe they are all asleep. After such an eventful night, I can't imagine being able to sleep at all. I stand still and listen for any type of movement or sound coming from the cabin. I can hear someone talking.

"Lettie," I call out, almost in a whisper. The talking stops.

"Lettie," I call out again. A few seconds later, the door swings open. Whoever it is doesn't have a candle and since its pitch black outside, I can't tell who it is.

"Lettie, is that you?"

"Yes it's me. Aggie? Why is you out here?" I inch closer.

"Can you come outside? I can't sleep." Lettie steps back inside her cabin, lights a candle and brings it outside. She's wearing one of those itchy looking night gowns like my mom. We both sit on her steps.

"How is your mom?" Lettie shakes her head.

"She finally restin' now. I could kill Massuh Raina for what he done." We sit there in uncomfortable silence for a few minutes, listening to the sounds of the night.

"You ever been to the main house? Where Nanny stay?"

"Yeah. Why?"

"I want to go and talk to Nanny."

"You not allowed to go up there. Nanny has to come down here."

"My Mom said I used to live up there with Nanny before. I don't see why I can't go up there," I say.

"Hmph, go on up there then. See what it get ya," Lettie snaps. I get the feeling she might be a little jealous that I used to live in the main house. I don't want her upset with me. She's my only friend here so if I want to try and get to freedom, I need my friend on my side.

"I got another secret," I say.

"What is it?" Lettie says dryly.

"I'm going to the main house to find a map so I can plan my escape up north."

"A girl can't escape by herself. You need a man to help you."

"A girl can do whatever a boy can do. Besides, I can read, can't nobody else around here read but me and the white folks."

"What if you get caught? You know what they do to young girls?"

"Lettie listen. Not only can I read, but I can write. I can write my own freedom papers. Sign Mr. Waters name on them and everything. I just need to get inside the main house so I can get some paper and an ink pen to write with. I can make it look official. All I need are freedom papers and a map." Lettie sits up straight, now interested in what I have to say.

"I didn't know you could write too."

"Of course I can write. So, how did you get that book? Did you steal it from the main house?"

"Shhhh!!!! I told mama Mistress Pippy give it to me. I snuck in there, late one night, they's all sleeping. Whole plantation sleepin' that night. Went in the study and grabbed it from the bookshelf. No one ever knew I was in there."

"Did you see pen and paper in the study?"

"I could barely see anything but I remember the moon was so bright that night. It was enough light I could find the books."

"You have to help me get in the study. I'm pretty sure there's paper and pen in there. Probably a map too."

"You think you just go back and work with Nanny again? Bet it be easy to get pen and paper if you already in the main house." Lettie has a point. Why not just go back with Nanny, work in the house. I can probably get anything I need then.

"You're so smart Lettie!"

"You write me freedom papers too so I's go wit' you?"

"Of course!"

"I's gon' be free! Just like my paw." Sadness sweeps down on us both.

"I'm so sorry about your daddy."

"All my fault. I's make my paw feel less of a man, talkin' all that stuff to him. Tell him take up for mama and be a man, don't let Massuh Raina do that to mama. All my fault."

"It's not your fault Lettie. Your daddy was trying to protect your mom, that's all."

"But I's the one tell him speak up for her. He told me let it be, like always. I couldn't let it be no mo'. Massuh Raina take my mama in that barn too many times. I know what he do to her in there. Paw always say 'Lettie stay away from Massuh Raina 'cause if he touch you I'd kill him.' Now my paw dead. He can't protect me or mama now." Lettie buries her face in her hands and her shoulders move up and down. Her cry is soft but sad enough to make me cry too. Regretfully, I think about those words I said to my dad, about him not being the man of the house and all. Lettie did the same thing, look what it got her daddy.

I touch Lettie's arm gently and she lifts her head.

"We're going to be free one day soon."

"Aggie, you have to do it soon. I's a feelin' Massuh Raina comin' for me now my paw gone. I seen the way he looked at me when I told Massuh Waters what happened. Somethin' bad gone happen if I don't leave here soon."

"Nanny should be here tomorrow for the funeral. I'll talk to her about moving back with her then. Unless I wake up in 2016 and this dream is over." I try cracking a joke but Lettie doesn't think it's funny. Little does she know, I'm just as serious as she is.

Chapter 11

Sleep leaves my body and I'm stirred awake by Mom clinking pots and pans. I'm still here in the year 1816. I've come to the conclusion I'm never leaving this place, unless I go through with my plan of escaping. At least if I can get up north, I can be free, go to school and get a real job. Maybe after working and making enough money I can come back and buy freedom for Mom. Mom is humming an unfamiliar tune and she's moving around better than yesterday. I guess her feet are feeling better.

I gather myself up from the floor and stretch. The floor is nowhere for a person to sleep. Even though my scar is healing on my back, my body aches from sleeping on the floor. Mom turns around and looks at me.

"Mornin' Aggie. Got our food ration today. Makin' you good breakfast, eggs, bacon even have flour for a couple of biscuits. Go on, sit down." Mama is scraping a pan of eggs onto a plate for me and her. The bacon looks a whole lot better than that salt pork stuff.

"How'd you make biscuits?"

"Went and used the brick oven down by Meyer's cabin. You know, ones cook all the food yest'day?"

"Oh yeah, where Phillip lives."

"Mmmm-hmmm." Mom continues to fuss about with the food. Not working today must have her in a good mood.

"Is Nanny coming over today?" I ask.

"'Spose to be. You thinkin' I forgot yo' birthday didn't you?"

"No, I completely forgot about my birthday actually."

"Nanny never let me forget yo' birthday. See, they has a calendar in the main house and every five month, we know your birthday come. Five month, thirteenth day."

"You know how to count?"

"Course I knows how to count. Jus' 'cause I can't read don't mean I can't count."

"Oh. Well, I want to ask Nanny if I can move back to the main house with her." I scrape the rest of my eggs off the plate with the heavy silver fork and stuff them in my mouth. I do whatever I can to keep from making eye contact with Mom since I know she won't like the idea of me leaving her.

"You don't want to stay here wit' me no mo'?"

"It's not that, I just need to learn a few more things from Nanny first. That's all."

"Oh, I see." Mom's demeanor changes from happy to sad.

"Mom, it's just for a little while. I think maybe going up there with Nanny it might help me get my memory back to normal. You said I lived there before right? That means I spent most of the time there with Nanny. I can't keep living like this, a 2016 girl in an 1816 world."

"Aggie, you were born in 1803. I don't understand this 2016 stuff you keep talkin' 'bout. You just need to get yo' head back right is all."

"Right, so maybe if I go and spend time with Nanny, around more familiar surroundings, that will help me get my head right. Then I can come back here with you. The sooner I get back to normal, the better."

"'Spose you right. Well, you has to get clean this evening, put on your good dress for Oscar's funeral." Mom moves the dishes from the shelf and pulls a loose brick from the wall. She reaches in the hole and pulls out a piece of soap wrapped in a linen napkin. There appears to be some papers in there too from what I can tell.

"Here, you can wash good with this soap. Fresh water in the bin for you." I walk over to Mom so I can get a good look in the hole.

"What else is in there?" I ask.

"Just some papers yo' daddy told me to keep. Don't really know what they is. A few coins he earned doing some side work as a blacksmith. Yo' daddy's always good wit' his hands, always providin' for us. Doing side work as a blacksmith he only made a few coins, not much but he save all he make. He said one day he's gone buy our freedom." I pull the papers from the hole. One of them is identical to the bounty Lettie carried in her book. The others spoke of the secret meetings with the abolitionists from up north. The papers also listed dates, times and locations for the meetings. As a matter of fact, one of them shows a meeting scheduled to take place the end of May, the 29th to be exact. I have to tell Lettie. We have two weeks to get things in order. Mom cocks her head to the side and squints her eyes.

"What's it say?" Mom asks.

"Talks about a secret meeting with a man who's an abolitionist from up north helping slaves trying to escape to freedom."

"Oh. Must be important to yo' daddy he had it in here. Go on and put it back. Massuh see something like this in here they whip all the skin off me. Your dress hanging over there." I notice the dress hanging on the hook and a pair of tie up boots below the dress on the floor. I guess this was considered our Sunday's best. Mom pulls open a burlap bag which I'm not real sure where she got it from, but inside she has a floppy looking hat. I want to tell her how ridiculous the hat looks and she'd look much better if she combed her hair, but the way she is trying to adjust the hat on her head I think I might hurt her feelings. Maybe this was the style for them on Sundays.

"Mom, why don't you let me comb your hair?"

"Don't really feel like fussin' wit' it today why I wanted to wear my hat." She adjusts the hat again, this time reminding me of Miss Celie from The Color Purple. How ironic, that's Mom's favorite movie, 2016 Mom that is.

I walk over to the barrel of water and touch it to see how cold it is. It didn't really matter, I was just happy to be able to wash some of the filth off my body. It was nice to have a piece of soap too. I continue to wash while Mom fusses about with her hat and hair. The dress on the hook is heavier than the dress I was wearing and has some extra layers at the bottom. The flowered pattern is hideous as is the ruffled collar and long sleeves. My sandy-colored hair is braid free and running wild. I try to tame it by putting it into a big ponytail. The good thing about it, I feel pretty. Not 2016, Easter Sunday, going to church pretty, but pretty.

I walk outside, giving Mom some privacy so she can wash up and get dressed. Other slaves have started to gather outside, everyone looking dapper in their best clothes. Even Ms. Louella is dressed up and instead of wearing a scarf on her head her long, mixed gray and black hair is pinned up in a bun. She is sitting in her favorite spot.

"Hi Grandma Lou. You look pretty. Been to church?"

"Thank you Aggie. Yes, jus' gettin' in from church. You look nice. Goin' to Oscar's funeral eh?"

"Yes ma'am. Have you seen Lettie?"

"Over yonder with Sylvie. They went to see Oscar's body one last time fo' he go in the ground."

"Oh." I wanted to ask more questions but I know Ms. Louella hates me to question her. Besides, Nanny and Mom told me if I needed to know something to ask them.

I wipe some of the dirt from the step before sitting beside Ms. Louella. Some of the slaves gathering don't look familiar to me. Maybe they are new to the plantation. I'll add that to my list of questions to ask Mom and Nanny. As if on queue, I see Nanny walking toward us. I run over and hug her tight.

"Hi Nanny!" I'm so happy to see her.

"Hi Aggie. Sho' look pretty today."

"Thank you Nanny."

"Before I forget, here." Nanny hands me a box. My birthday present - I forgot. Tears well up in my eyes when I think about the bunny card and the $50 bill Nanny gave me for my birthday in 2016. She always remembers my birthday, even in 1816.

"What is it?"

"Open it chile." I open the box, revealing a handmade bracelet made of twine and a butterfly charm made of steel.

"Yo' daddy made that fo' ya. Wanted to surprise ya wit' it fo they moved him. Gave it to me and say 'Make sho' you give this to Aggie'. He always do somethin' special fo' you and yo' mama. Me too. He a good boy. I raise him right." Nanny has tears running down her cheeks. I put my bracelet on and hug her tight. I miss my Dad.

☐

Slaves from other plantations were given permission to attend Oscar's funeral. At nightfall, the funeral procession began and we all march down the hill behind Sylvie, Lettie and the rest of their family. The slaves all hum and sing negro spirituals until we arrive at the cemetery. Mister Rainer and another white man on a horse seem to be chaperoning the entire event, I guess to make sure no one gets out of line. How unfair for him to be here since he's the one to cause Oscar's death. I'm sure Sylvie is not happy about it but I'm beginning to learn a lot about how things work around here. Slaves' feelings don't matter, not ever. Slaves aren't even considered people, just property. That's just the way it is.

At the cemetery, the singing gets louder and everyone is rejoicing. Sylvie and the kids are sad but everyone else celebrates the fact Oscar is no longer here on the plantation. He is finally free. It's sort of eerie to me, being in a cemetery at night but Nanny says this is the only time slaves have free time to celebrate life which is at night especially Sunday night since slaves don't work on Sundays.

The wooden box holding Oscar's body looks nothing like the casket my other grandma was buried in. I bet all kinds of animals and insects from underground will get into that box easy. The thought makes me cringe. I'm glad the box is closed and has been put in the hole dug by the other slaves. They even started covering the box with dirt already. As funeral goers continue singing, Sylvie, Lettie and the other kids are placing some of Oscar's things on his grave: A pipe, a cup, different hand tools, and a scarf.

"Nanny, why are they doing that?" I whisper.

"Keep the spirit happy." Nanny continues singing. I don't know what that means.

"Whose spirit?" I ask.

"Oscar." More singing from Nanny and I still don't understand what she means.

When Sylvie and her family are done putting mementos on the grave, the funeral procession heads up the hill back to the slave quarters where all of the families have pitched in and prepared food which is laid out buffet style over by Phillip's family's cabin. The singing continues and someone has started to play a drum. What we refer to as a repast in 2016 is happening now.

People have started dancing and singing more songs but these songs are more uplifting.

Boy oh boy did they put out a spread of food. A lot of the slaves from the other plantations brought food, even different kinds of desserts.

The children are all running around, some of them have joined hands and are playing a game which reminds me of Ring around the Rosy. Today, which is supposed to be a day of sadness is the day I've seen people the happiest. I stand off in the distance just watching everyone. This is the third day I've been here but it feels like a lifetime.

Chapter 12

It wasn't hard convincing Nanny to let me move back to the slave quarters at the main house but her convincing Mr. Waters was my concern. I was amazed he allowed it with no questions asked which is odd to me since he was the one who let Mr. Rainer give me a lashing. Then I thought about what Mom said about Mr. Waters' daddy being my granddaddy. Maybe that's why Nanny has been working in the house her whole life and she tends to live better than Mom.

Leaving the grounds of the slave quarters of the field slaves, I immediately know when I'm nearing the main house because the grass is thick and green and there are flowers blooming everywhere. The graveled entranceway is long and wide, lined with short bushes which are currently being trimmed by a few slaves. They all seem to know who I am, nodding and saying hello as I get closer to the big house. When I say big, I mean big. I count three rows of oversized windows, two porches stacked on top of each other which appear to be held up by oversized columns. This all brick mansion boasts a sprawling brick staircase leading up to the main entrance. Sticking out like a thorn to the right of the main house is a smaller building with only two windows. Even though the building is attached to the main house, it is not all brick. Instead it is red just like the big barn. On instinct, I walk toward the smaller building. I know a slave is not supposed to go into the main entrance of some white person's house if we can't even look them in the eye when we talk. I slow my pace to watch as some slaves work the yard, cutting the grass, pruning flowers and plants and female slaves are on the porches sweeping and wiping windows. The door to the main entrance opens so I freeze in my tracks. Mr. Waters appears along with a white woman wearing a dress that's so wide at the bottom I swear she has two small children hidden underneath. Her waist is tiny, looks like she's been wearing a waist trainer her entire life. The mid length sleeves on her dress are adorned with lots of lace as is the short neckline which seems to smother her breasts so much I don't think she can breathe too good. Her hair is partially pinned up while sections are cascading in ringlets of golden curls. She has a very pretty face. I'm assuming she must be Ms. Pippy but I'm not 100% sure. As big as this house is, there has to be more than one family living here.

"Aggie, make sure Nanny gets you cleaned up good ya hear"?

"Yes Master Waters." I'm not sure if I'm supposed to acknowledge the woman - curtsy, bow or something. I just make sure I don't look at either of them like Nanny said.

"Welcome back Aggie," says the lady. What am I supposed to call her? I don't know who she is!

"Thank you ma'am." The best I could come up with. I stand there, waiting for them to go back inside but they stand there, waiting for me to get where I need to be. Them watching me makes me nervous because I don't want to go the wrong way or do the wrong thing. About a foot away from me a slave is pruning a large shrub and he notices my confusion. He tilts his head to the left, directing me with his eyes. I'm not sure if I can go or if I need Mr. Waters to tell me first.

"Can I go now Master Waters?"

"Yes, go on now gal."

I follow the man's eyes around the side of the house to the red house. Once out of eye view of Mr. Waters, I take a deep breath. I start to explore more, taking in the beauty of the grounds. As I near the rear of the house, I see a gazebo with a sitting area, an abundance of trees and pathways which lead to a pond. More slaves tend to the back yard and I notice there is a wraparound porch on the big house. The door opens to the small, red house and Nanny appears.

"Aggie, why you standin' out there daydreamin', come on in hea."

Nanny is wearing a head wrap, black dress and apron. Inside, there are a couple of bunk style beds lining two of the walls. In the middle of the room is a rectangular shaped, wooden table and wood benches on each side. The fireplace is surrounded by lots of shelves which are filled with dishes, pots and pans, and some other items I'm not too sure of. The floor is all wood, there are a few small pieces of furniture scattered about which are covered with cloth. I don't know how many people stay in here but it's definitely an upgrade compared to the cabins in the slave quarters where Mom and Lettie live. No wonder Lettie had an attitude when I mentioned coming to live up here. Everything is neat an orderly, there's even a tall wardrobe in the corner where clothes are hung.

"We gotsta get you cleaned up. Hea', take this dress and these shoes, go on over and wash up. Massuh don't like house slaves to be dirty. Befo' you set one foot in his house you hasta be clean. Wash good now."

I take off my three-day dress and do as Nanny tells me. She hands me another long dress, floral print and plain, but clean and pressed. I slip on the dress after washing up and Nanny ties an apron around my waist.

"You's gotta cover your hair. Hea'," she covers my head with a wrap like hers. She tries to tame the curly sandy hair on my head, which, if I was still in 2016, it would be braided. But for some reason my natural hair is running wild in 1816. The little things lacking for

Mom, Nanny has at her fingertips – Nice pieces of soap, a comb and brush, even a bed to sleep on.

"Why on earth would I leave here to go and live down there? You got it good up here Nanny."

"Let me tell you somethin' chile. Up hea, you on call all day and night, e'vry day. No time off. When Massuh call, you come. It don't matter how early or late. We either waitin' on Mistress Pippy, or her two chil'ren, or Massuh Waters. If they wants anything, we gotsta do it. Don't make it out to be heaven hea 'cause it ain't."

"I'd rather do this than work in those fields all day."

"We'll see. Hurry up. I's gotta show you around since yo' head still ain't right. Massuh get wind you lost all yo' memory he might send you back wit' yo' mama."

I follow Nanny up a narrow stairway which connects to the kitchen of the main house. The kitchen reminds me of one of those from a cooking show, long countertops, lots of cabinets and pots and pans hanging from the ceiling. A fireplace appears to take up an entire wall. There are two other slaves in the kitchen dressed like Nanny preparing food.

"Welcome back Aggie," they both say to me. I just smile and say hi. Of course I don't remember them.

"Dis hea is the slave kitchen, where's we prepare food for the Waters," Nanny whispers to me.

Once out of the kitchen we go down a long hallway, with shiny hardwood floors, high ceilings and walls covered in wall paper. Family photos line the walls and we pass a door that's closed, I assume it's off limit to us. Nanny leads me to the formal dining room, which has seating for ten people, a brass chandelier with long candles and drapes that look like they weigh a ton. This room also has a china cabinet, a wood serving table and another small, long cabinet which is adorned with crystal trinkets and other knickknacks. The table is covered with a lace tablecloth and there's a china place setting for each seat.

"This the dining room. You has to shine the crystal and dust e'vry day in here. In this cabinet is the silver. E'vry otha day, polish silver. Massuh Waters real stickler for clean. No dust on the floor, tables, nowheres. Best thing fo' ya is to shake them drapes first, then do yo' dustin. Sweep and polish the flo' last. Dining room has to be done befo' suppa. They only eat dinner here. I's show you where they eat breakfast and lunch."

There are two entrances to the dining room and Nanny takes me through the one which leads to the open foyer where the entrance door is and a winding staircase. I've never seen so much hardwood in my life. There's another chandelier in the ceiling of the foyer, but this one is the mother of all chandeliers. There's a living room on the opposite side of the formal dining room. Both the dining room and living room are accented with huge columns. I peek my head in the living room then I see it - adjacent to the living room is the study with ceiling to floor bookshelves and a wood desk and chair.

"Livin' room, study and bedrooms handled by Maureen and Emy. We handle kitchens, dinin' rooms, and all the cooking. You and me wait on Mistress Pippy and Massuh Waters, Maureen and Emy handle the chil'ren."

"Do we ever switch up duties sometimes?"

"Only if Massuh wants a switch. Aggie listen, do as you's told. Don't go questionin' nobody, ya hea? You talk to me if you has questions. I know you still sick in the head a bit. Maureen and Emy get wind you not right they tell Massuh, gets me and you in trouble."

"Yes ma'am."

Nanny completes the tour of the house and explaining my chores. I wish I could write everything down so I don't forget but I know I can't do that. A smile creeps across my face. At least now I know where the ink and paper is. My freedom papers will be written very soon.

My work starts immediately and I try to remember everything Nanny told me I was responsible for. This reminds me of getting up on Saturday morning, Mom yelling to get out of bed so we can clean the house. I wonder what Mom is doing right now. I hope she's not too sad without me. I wish I could tell her my plan but I can't because it would put her in jeopardy of getting in trouble. Lettie and I made a promise to keep our secret and in two weeks, if I'm still here, we will be on our way to freedom.

Chapter 13

My first night working in the main house goes off without a hitch. I confirmed the lady on the front porch with the really big dress was definitely Ms. Pippy and met her two children, Joseph and Heather. Heather appears to be about my age and she's really fond of me. Such a shame I have no recollection of her. Her brother Joseph is younger and he acts a lot like Mr. Rainer instead of his own father - real mean and obnoxious. I have to stay clear of him.

Me, Nanny, Maureen and Emy all sleep in the bunk beds. Nanny explained there is a small cabin behind the house where the slaves live that work the grounds. Sometimes, when Mr. and Mrs. Waters held dinner parties, those slaves clean up and help Maureen, Emy and Nanny serve guests. I guess I'm part of the serving crew now. Well, I won't be for long.

I don't waste a lot of time getting what I need from the study. I had to get those papers written as well as find a map so me and Lettie can get a good enough start. Those meetings are held in Richmond which is about 35 miles from where we are in Goochland County. Not a lot if you had a car, but a long way when you have to do it by foot.

As hard as it's been, I have been up for hours, lying in bed waiting for the time to creep by. My eyelids are as heavy as the day is long, but I force myself to stay awake all night so I can go into the study while everyone is asleep. Nanny's snoring almost feels like a lullaby, hypnotizing me into slumber, but I fight it. Being on the top bunk, I'm hoping my movement won't wake the others. I move in slow motion, off the bed and across the room to the entrance to the kitchen. When I get to the top of the stairs, I notice a door I hadn't noticed before. It must've been open when Nanny gave me the tour. My heart beats fast when I turn the knob. I just know the door is going to squeak when I open it. Sweat builds on my hands, under my arms and on my back. I put one hand on the door and the other on the knob and open it, little by little. Holding my breath through the entire process, I exhale once the door is open wide enough for me to slip through. Lucky for me, the moon is bright tonight, which is another reason I had to act quickly. Without a candle, it would probably be pitch black walking through this house. However, the large windows allow the moonlight to illuminate each room.

I tiptoe through the kitchen, down the hall until I'm in the foyer directly in front of the winding staircase. I can feel my heart beating through my chest. For a moment, I stand frozen, listening for any sign of movement in the upstairs bedrooms. A few of the windows are open and outside the sounds from crickets and frogs help to drown out my fear. I make my way to the study and look around. Even with the moonlight, it's hard to see but I make out the bottle of ink with the feather sticking out of it and paper on the desk. The paper is very thick, feels almost like construction paper. I panic when I realize there's only one bottle of ink on the desk. I need to see if there is any extra around I can take and it go undetected. Opening the drawer proved to be another challenge. I wipe the sweat from my hands and open the top drawer slowly. There is more ink and writing paraphernalia, thank goodness. I grab what I need from the drawer, some paper and close the drawer. The walk back to the slave quarters seems to be longer than before as I tiptoe back.

Once I'm back, Nanny's snoring indicates all is well. The burlap sap I used to store my old dress proves to be a perfect hiding spot. I let out a heavy sigh of relief when I'm back on the top bunk. Mission accomplished.

Chapter 14

Here I am on day four as a slave. As time continues to move on, I'm starting to accept the fact I won't be returning to my old life. Maybe God has punished me for being a spoiled, ungrateful, disrespectful brat. Nanny always says God can do anything. Well, he certainly turned my life around. This nightmare and dream has gone on long enough and it's obvious I'm not getting out of it. Stuff like this happens in the movies. Movies are supposed to be fiction but there must be some truth to them. I'm here aren't I?

Two hours of sleep has done me no good as I can barely function. Luckily, the Waters family is gone to Powhatan County for some sort of fair. The bad news is Mr. Waters left Mr. Rainer in charge as head overseer. He's only been in the house once so far today, to make sure everyone is working.

Nanny and I are in the kitchen preparing food should the Waters' want something to eat when they return. She's also giving me a good lesson on how to properly shine silver.

Maureen and Emy use this time to wash linen and they come downstairs with an armload to wash.

Emy, who looks to be about twenty-one, is eyeing me pretty hard.

"What's wrong Emy?" I ask.

"Come with me Aggie. I's like to talk to you in private," says Emy.

"Jus' 'cause Massuh not hea don't get no ideas Emy. Aggie has to do her own chores," says Nanny.

"Yes'm." I follow Emy outside to the back yard where there is a wash bucket set up. She puts the linen in a basket beside the wash bucket before she starts handwashing the linen in the big bucket.

"Well? What is it?" I ask.

"I knows what you did last night," Emy says. I swallow hard.

"What are you talking about?"

"If'n you don't put the stuff back, I's going straight to Massuh and tell him what you done. I won't take blame fo' yo' stealing," says Emy.

"I'm not stealing. I just borrowed it. I'm putting it back when I finish."

"You needs to put it back now 'fore Massuh come home. He finds out, I's in trouble, not you. Study is my area to keep clean, so he gone 'cuse me." How in the world did she know what was missing? I took the ink from the drawer. And who counts paper anyway?

"Please Emy. I just need a couple of days to write my

letters then I'll return the ink and stuff. Please!"

"Should I tell Nanny what you done? I tells Nanny or I tells Massuh. You choose. Either way, it goes back 'fore Massuh come home tonight." My head throbs from the dilemma I'm in.

"How do you know I have it?"

"I's up when you came back from the study last night. I saw you put it in your bag. I don't sleep much, you needs to know that." Emy's skin is a pretty bronze color and her eyes are like marbles. Her blonde hair makes her look like a white woman with a tan. I bet she wouldn't have any trouble getting to freedom. Then I had an idea.

"Emy, you want to be free?" Emy looks at me and rolls her eyes.

"I'm serious. I have a plan and if you want to be part of it, we could walk off this plantation and never look back." Emy looks around to see who might be watching us. Talk of freedom has a way of getting a slave's attention.

"What's this plan Aggie?"

"Do you realize you can pass for a white woman?" I say.

"So?"

"Well, I was going to write freedom papers for me and Lettie, but if you want to escape with us, I can write papers that say you are our owner. You can get one of Mrs. Waters' dresses, get yourself dolled up and

if someone tries to stop us, you can say you're white."
Emy chuckles.

"Nanny said you was crazy in the head and now I believe her. You is crazy girl!"

"Have you seen yourself? Your hair is just as blonde as Pippy Waters."

"You don't have no right callin' her name that way. You gone' get whipped or worse."

"Emy, your eyes, your hair even your skin."

"My skin not white like hers," Emy snaps.

"I know, but it just looks like you've been in the sun, at the beach and you got a tan. If anybody questions it, you can say you've been at the beach."

"Aggie, put the stuff back before Massuh return. I have work to do." I guess that was her way of dismissing me.

"Just think about it," I say before going back into the house. Nanny is still mixing something in a bowl and the silver is on the counter waiting for me.

"What Emy wants wit' you?" Nanny asks.

"Nothing. I think she thought I was going to help her with that washing." I hate lying to Nanny but if I tell her I put her in jeopardy of getting in trouble if someone finds out.

I continue with shining the silver while Nanny cooks, humming a tune.

"Nanny, I need to see Mom. Can I go and see her today?"

"Yo' mama is in the fields now, won't be done 'til sundown. By then Massuh be home and need us serve him and his family." I need to come up with another lie.

"What about Lettie? She in the fields too?"

"Lettie might be working at the barn, tending the animals. If'n you go over there, you don't wear yo' house clothes ya' hear? And you come back 'fore sundown. Alls yo' work finished right?"

"Soon as I'm done with this silver it will be."

"Go on and hurry back. Stay outta Massuh Raina's way." I put the silver polish away and take the silver back to the dining room. After storing it in its' rightful place, I rush down to the slave quarters to get changed. I pull my old dress from the burlap sack, careful not to pull the writing supplies out in the process. After hanging my house clothes on a hook on the wall, I hurry outside towards the barn. I run through the grass as swarms of gnats hit me in the face. When I get to the barn, I spot Lettie feeding some chickens.

"Lettie!" I yell. She turns and puts her hand over her eyes to shade the sun. When she realizes it's me, she runs over.

"Aggie! What you doin' here?"

"I got the stuff Lettie. But I have to return it or that heffa Emy is going to squeal on me." Lettie looks confused. 2016 slang means nothing to her.

"Emy knows I took the writing stuff. She told me she

was going to tell Mr. Waters if I don't return it tonight. I have to write the letters today so I can put the stuff back. Anybody in the barn?"

"No, not right now. Phillip was in there tendin' to the horses but he jus' left."

"I'll go in there and write the letters. You keep an eye out for me. Yell if someone comes."

"OK." Lettie continues feeding the chickens while I push open the heavy door to the barn. The stench of the horses hit me first so I cover my nose and mouth with my hand.

I look around for a place to sit, settling on a large mound of hay pushed in the corner of the barn. After grabbing a piece of plywood to bear down on, I pull out the writing supplies. All this talk about freedom papers and I have no idea what to write on a freedom letter. Even worse, I don't know Mr. Waters' first name. I'm pretty sure his full name needs to be on the paper. I guess I just have to wing it. The papers aren't legit so it won't matter if the full name is right or not. Then again, it might make more sense to make up the full name of the slave owner so it will be hard to track us down. I like that idea.

After writing my idea of what I think a freedom letter should look like, I fold both pieces of paper and stuff them back in the burlap sack. Using the ink and feather are new for me so there's some ink on my hand. I'll have to hide my hand until I'm able to wash it off.

Feeling ten feet tall, I march out the barn as if my freedom is tattooed on my chest. I just need to find a map and me and Lettie will be planning our move.

I stop in my tracks when I notice Mr. Rainer accosting Lettie. He's all up in her face and she's trying her best to get around him. I drop the bag on the ground and kick it back inside the barn.

"Lettie, you need help?" I ask, hoping Mr. Rainer will ease up.

They both turn to look at me, Lettie with fear in her eyes, Mr. Rainer with lust in his.

"Does it look like she needs help?" says Mr. Rainer who has his filthy hands on Lettie's chin. Lettie is trying her best not to cry.

"I was going to help her with feeding the animals, that's all, Master Rainer." Mr. Rainer pushes Lettie out the way and walks toward me.

"Did I ask you anything gal?"

"No sir." I look down at my feet, trying hard not to look at him directly.

"Stay in yo' place then. Thought you'd learn that by now. I's just tellin' Lettie she startin' to look mo' and mo' like her mammy. Sho is a pretty gal." He walks over to touch Lettie again when Phillip appears, running and out of breath.

"Massuh Raina sir, Massuh Lee say he needs you down by the fields." Talk about perfect timing. Mr. Rainer pauses before jumping on his horse and riding toward the fields. Phillip runs over to hug Lettie who bursts into tears. Before going to console my friend, I grab my bag from the barn.

"I's gotsta get away from here. Not too long 'fore he tries to take me in that barn," cries Lettie.

"I's kill him if he hurts you Lettie. I promise, I won't let him hurt you," says Phillip.

"How? My own paw couldn't protect me or mama. You just a boy. Best thing for me is to go." Lettie wipes her tears on the back of her hand. Phillip's shoulders slump when Lettie pulls away from him. Poor Phillip. He really cares about Lettie.

"Lettie, I have to go back to the main house and get changed before Mr. Waters gets back. You think you can make it one more day?"

"One mo' day? You promise?"

"Yep. Should have everything I need then everything is all set." Phillip looks from Lettie to me then back to Lettie again.

"Y'all tryin' to escape ain't ya?"

"No such thing," Lettie says, not really convincing. I avoid the question all together.

"I'll see you tomorrow Lettie. Bye Phillip." I run back towards the main house, feeling reenergized. The adrenaline I'm feeling trumps the tiredness I had from the two hours of sleep I got last night. When I get to the backyard of the main house, I slow down to keep from bringing attention to myself. Emy is still washing linen, pushing sheets around in the big wash bucket with a wooden paddle. When she sees me, her lips tighten. I smirk at her before heading inside.

I put my "house" clothes back on, stuffing my old dress into the burlap sack and wrapping the letters inside the dress. I tuck the ink and feather beneath my apron, then I notice the ink on my hand. Getting the ink back in the drawer should be easy since the Waters are not home yet. Emy is outside so I don't have to worry about her snooping around.

I go upstairs and Nanny is still in the kitchen which is sweltering from all the cooking she's been doing. Beads of sweat cover her forehead and for a moment, Nanny doesn't notice me.

"Hi Nanny," I say.

"Have fun wit' Lettie? Needs yo' help in here. Waters family be home soon."

"OK. I need to go to the dining room for a second. I think I forgot to do something in there."

"OK, hurry up chile."

I head over to the dining room then make a beeline to the study. It's so much easier during daylight to really see everything in the study. The writing supplies are put back in their rightful place, minus the paper I used. There has to be a map around here somewhere. My eyes scan the room. Nothing. Maybe there's one in the drawer. Before I can get the drawer open, I hear Maureen coming down the stairs. In a panic, I hide under the desk. It would've made more sense just to walk out of the room, but my guilty conscious got the best of me. Maureen is in the living room doing light dusting, humming to herself. I watch as her feet walk over the large rug since the study is adjacent to the living room. Her humming stops, she hesitates then walks over to the window.

"Nanny, they's back!" she yells. Oh my God. Maureen needs to get out of the living room so I can make a run for the kitchen before the Waters family walks in. My heart feels like it's in my throat and the air around me seems to dissipate. What in the world would happen to me if they caught me in here? To make matters worse, I still have this ink on my hand.

Maureen hurries down the hallway, giving me enough time to come from under the desk. Or so I thought. As I'm about to exit the study, I nearly bump into Joseph. For an eight-year-old, he's not that big, but I can feel the hatred seeping through his pores.

"Nigger gal, what you doin' in my daddy's study? You don't belong in there."

"I, I, I was helping Maureen and Emy with the cleaning, that's all. Emy had a lot of linen to wash so I just thought I'd help her out." The front door swings open and Mr. Waters and Ms. Pippy enter. Heather is behind them.

"What's going on here Joseph?" Mr. Waters ask.

"I just caught this gal coming out your study

Father."

"Aggie, you want to explain yourself?" Just then, Maureen comes down the hallway to greet the Waters family. She looks at me strange.

"I was just telling Joseph that I was helping Maureen and Emy with some dusting in the study, that's all. Right Maureen?" Maureen has a look of confusion on her face. She has no idea what's going on, but whatever it is she wasn't going to be thrown under the bus for it. With my eyes, I try pleading with Maureen to go along with the story.

"Is that right Maureen?" asks Ms. Pippy. The long silence should've been a dead giveaway.

"I didn't ask fo' no help Massuh. Emy and me do our own chores just fine."

Why were these slaves so loyal to people who would whip them and sell them off at the drop of the dime?

"Aggie, I don't take kindly to liars. You want to tell me why you were really in my study?" ask Mr. Waters. The back of my ears are on fire and sweat is rolling down my back. Maureen won't look at me but everybody else is.

"Honestly, Master Waters, I wanted to see the globe. It's so pretty. That's all." Trying hard to keep my hands out of view, I keep them hidden in my apron pockets. Joseph tends to be the only one who notices.

"Father, I think she may have something in her pocket." I hate that little boy. Why does he have it in for me?

"Aggie, a liar is one thing, but a thief? Please tell me you haven't stolen anything from me."

"Oh no Master Waters. I didn't steal anything, honest. You can check your study to see if anything is missing. I just wanted to look at the globe, that's it."

"If that is true, take your hands from your pockets." I give Joseph the side eye before clenching my hands into fists and removing them from my pockets.

"You want to open them?" says Mr. Waters. I open my hands with the palm facing the floor. I can feel my heartbeat in my mouth. Joseph puts his hands in my pockets, searching for something that isn't there. I'm praying they won't ask me to turn my hands over. After being frisked by Joseph, Mr. Waters and Ms. Pippy appear to be relieved Joseph came up empty. I don't take Mr. Waters as the kind who like to discipline slaves, but he doesn't mind giving the task to someone else.

"Joseph, upstairs you go. It's time to get ready for supper. Go on with Maureen. Heather, the same goes for you," says Ms. Pippy.

"Oh Mother," Heather exclaims before marching up the stairs behind Maureen and Joseph.

"Aggie, I'll be keeping my eye on you. I know your grandmother raised you well," says Ms. Pippy before she lifts her humongous dress in the front and walks up the stairs, leaving me standing there with Mr.

Waters. By now, Nanny has come from the kitchen and is standing in the foyer looking at me and Mr. Waters. His back is to her so he doesn't see her.

"Aggie, your grandmother means the world to me. But I will only tell you this one time. If I find out you are lying or stealing, I will ship you off to another plantation, just like your daddy. I have no tolerance for either one. You hear?"

"Yes Master Waters."

"And since when have you started speaking so well?"

"I don't know what you mean?"

"Massuh Waters, I hopes Aggie not givin' ya no trouble," Nanny says.

He turns to face Nanny who immediately looks down at her hands.

"No Nanny, no trouble at all. Right Aggie?"

"Yes sir."

"We'll be getting ready for supper shortly Nanny." Mr. Waters disappears up the stairs. When he is out of range, Nanny grabs me by the arm.

"What is you doin'? I's already told you this area's Maureen's and Emy's. Why you in hea? Come on," Nanny pushes me down the hallway toward the kitchen.

"Wait Nanny. I need to go outside."

"Aggie, we has work to do. Massuh and Mistress don't like waitin' on they food."

"Just going to the outhouse. Be right back." I go down the backstairs to the slave quarters. Luckily Emy's not there so I use the wash bucket and scrub the ink from my hand. It's not coming off as fast as I'd like but I keep scrubbing until there is no trace of it. I turn around and Nanny is staring at me.

"What you did Aggie?"

"Nothing Nanny, I just needed to wash my hands. That's all." Nanny comes closer and notices the ink on the sponge.

"What is 'dis?"

"I don't know, just got on my hand when I went to the farm with Lettie..." The smack stings my lips. I put my hand to my face, shocked that Nanny hit me. Tears well up in my eyes. Nanny has never hit me before. Even as a little kid, she never disciplined me for anything.

"Nanny??!" I cry.

"You think I's stupid? You's in Massuh writing ink won't ya? Yo' mama told me you can write. Saw where you scribbled yo' name in the dirt by the cabin. What you tryin' to do Aggie?"

"Nothing."

"Don't lie to me chile. I ain't stupid. Aggie, tell me the truth right now!" I look Nanny in the eyes. I've never seen her so angry – Never. Lying to her is not an option. I grab my burlap sack.

"What you doin'?" Nanny asks. I unfold my dress

and reveal the freedom papers. Nanny grabs the papers, looking at them like she can read them.

"You can read?" I ask.

"I can read a little. You tryin' to get to freedom wit' these?"

"Yes."

"You wanna be strung up on a tree? Fool chile these won't work. Freedom papers has to be filed at da courthouse. Whose Massuh name you got hea?"

"I made it up. I'm sorry Nanny, but I have to get away from here."

"Oh Aggie. Sit down a minute." Nanny walks to the fireplace reaches for one of the top shelves and slides it out. There is a small, tin box inside about the size of a sardine can. Inside there's a piece of paper, folded several times to fit into the box. Nanny hands the paper to me. I can't even classify this writing style as cursive writing but I try to make out what I can by reading the paper several times. It takes me a moment but I finally grasp what I'm reading.

"You're free?" I ask.

"Yes. Been free since I's turn fifty-years-old. Elder Massuh Waters promise me my freedom when I turn 50 and he did the same fo' yo' daddy. Elder Massuh Waters sweet on me since I come here. Never had me move no wheres else once I got here. Yo' daddy and young Massuh Waters brothers." It takes me a minute to comprehend what Nanny said. That means Mr.

Waters, the same Mr. Waters who ordered Mr. Rainer to whip me, is my uncle. Can this dream get anymore twisted?

"Nanny, if you're free, why are you still here as a slave?"

"Can't leave my fam'ly. My boy, you and Sandra only fam'ly I knows. Besides, yo' daddy had a plan. He's gone buy his freedom and come fo' you and yo' mama. He couldn't wait 'til he's fifty. We's all leave here togetha' one day. But somethin' happen Fr'day. I don't know why young Massuh Waters sell yo' daddy like he did. He never like yo' daddy much. Maybe 'cause his daddy made him. Always kind to me though in a strange way. I guess 'cause his momma so mean to me when she's living. Plus I's his wet nurse when he's born." I stare at Nanny's freedom papers again. My letters look nothing like this. There is no way someone would believe us if we showed those fake letters. The penmanship is so different and the writing read like someone from England wrote it. The most important piece was the seal of approval from the courthouse.

"Since Dad is gone, why don't you try and leave now, go look for him. You have freedom papers, you can do that right?"

"Not so simple Aggie. Just 'cause I got freedom papers don't mean I's really free. I walk down that road, all alone, first white man see me try to have his way wit me then hang me from a tree for thinkin' I's better than them."

"What about the abolitionist? Can't he help you?"

"Where I's going? Too old to start ova somewhere's else. My life hea not so bad. Young Massuh Waters respect me. His family too. Only 'cause his daddy cared about me and my boy 'fore he died."

"But Nanny, I don't want to be a slave. I want to be free too. I don't want my mom to be a slave either. Her life is so much harder than yours and mine. And I want to find my dad." Tears are streaming down my cheeks.

"I know Aggie, I know. Jus' the way the world is. Freedom to me is just a piece of paper." Nanny hugs me tight, just like the bunny on the birthday card. I cry harder. I want to go home.

Chapter 15

Day five of slavery. Waking up as a slave has become a norm to me. I guess when we are put in certain situations we learn to adapt. Nanny shot down all of my dreams of becoming a free slave since I can't seem to get out of this nightmare. It's strange though. 2016 Nanny always told me to go for it, never give up, the sky's the limit, all that good stuff. 1816 Nanny is the complete opposite. Is it because she's stuck? Stuck in a life she doesn't know how to get out of? How could you have freedom handed to you and you not take it and run? It doesn't make much sense to me. I mean, I understand not wanting to leave your family because I can't imagine going on with my life without my family. But having the opportunity of a lifetime and not take it just doesn't make sense to me.

I turn over on the hard bunk bed, trying to scratch my back where the scab is starting to peel from my lashing. Today I'll have to deliver the bad news to Lettie. Our letters aren't worth the paper they're written on. If anything we'd probably get hung for drafting such a fraudulent letter. In a way, I'm glad Nanny saw the letters. Nanny, Maureen and Emy are still sleeping. A slight breeze blows through the window and the birds are chirping a melody. It's only during this time that I feel normal when the world is still.

Sadness consumes me when I think of Mom and Dad. I wonder what Dad did to Mr. Waters to be sold off to another plantation? Especially since he's Mr. Waters' half-brother? Maybe he got wind that Dad was trying to escape. Dad is smart, good with his hands and would've found a way to freedom eventually.

When the door swings open, we all jump up in bed, startled. It's Mr. Rainer. This can't be good.

"Get up all of you, right now." We do as we're told, wondering why Mr. Rainer is in the slave quarters so early in the morning.

"Aggie, get over here." I jump from the top bunk and walk over to Mr. Rainer.

"Where's yo' bag?"

"What bag?"

"Don't sass me gal, you know what bag I'm talkin' 'bout. The burlap sack you keep your letters in." My eyes get as big as golf balls. How did he know about the letters?

"I don't have a bag with any letters in it." What else was I supposed to say? There's no way I would volunteer any information and throw myself under the bus. He wants a bag with some letters, let him find it. Out the corner of my eye, I see my bag, in plain view, hanging on the hook. There's another bag hanging on a hook too which belongs to Emy. The letters are still wrapped in my old dress inside the bag. Mr. Rainer looks around, eyeing our meager belongings.

"Emy, show me Aggie's bag." I lock eyes with Emy. She's probably glad to turn me in and doesn't waste time grabbing my bag from the hook on the wall. Mr. Rainer snatches the bag from Emy and pulls everything from it. He shakes the dress and the letters fall to the ground. Maureen lets out a loud gasp but Emy doesn't seem to be surprised. I bet she's the one who snitched.

Mr. Rainer opens the letters, reading them to himself. The grin on his face is wicked almost like the devil.

"Tsk, tsk, tsk. You wanna tell me who wrote these?"

"No."

"What did you say gal?"

"I said no! I don't want to tell you who wrote them. You know who wrote them. Just do what you have to do to me. Whip me, sell me, hang me, I don't care anymore. Anything is better than living this life. I know because I had a better life before this." Mr. Rainer punches me in the stomach then grabs me by the arm.

"Oh yeah, Mr. Waters will want to hear all about this. Come on." He drags me up the stairs through the kitchen. Nanny is following behind us, crying softly, pleading for my life.

"Mr. Waters! Mr. Waters!" Mr. Rainer's yelling is so loud, the pictures on the walls in the hallway are shaking. He grabs me until we are in the foyer at the foot of the stairs. Mr. Waters' bedroom door opens and he appears, clad in nightclothes. He tries to put on his robe while coming down the stairs.

"Rainer?! Do you know what time it is? This better be important." Mr. Rainer pushes me toward Mr. Waters, so hard I almost fall to the ground.

"This gal had plans of escaping the plantation and taking Lettie wit' her. She wrote fake freedom papers. I guess she got the supplies from your study. Joseph told me all about catching her in your study. She's been sneaking around writin' letters, planning an escape. Here," Mr. Rainer hands the letters to Mr. Waters. Nanny stands silent, terror in her eyes, hands on her face in despair. Mr. Waters scan the letters.

"Aggie? You got something to say about this?" I look at Nanny. Already free but scared of freedom.

"No."

"Mr. Waters, lemme handle her. I'll take care of her real fine," says Mr. Rainer.

"That will be all for now Mr. Rainer. I'll take it from here."

"But don't you want me to teach her a lesson?"

"Yes and you will. But I need to talk to Nanny and Aggie privately first."

"I'll be right out front." Mr. Rainer exits through the front door. I have a lump in my throat. The angst is killing me.

"Step into the living room." We follow behind Mr. Waters. He walks over to a cabinet and pours himself a drink.

"Nanny, why are you still here?"

"'Cuse me Massuh?"

"You have been free for almost fifteen years, yet you're still here. Why is that?"

"Guess 'cause I has nowhere to go. Plus my family's here, well what's left of it."

"My father made me promise to look after you and that son of yours. On his deathbed, I promised him I would."

"Yes, I know. He said I could stay as long as I want. Why you say all this Massuh Waters? My heart is aching. Can you just say what you gon' do to Aggie?"

"I say all this because, sometimes I'm sweet on you, then there are times I despise you and yours. But I feel obligated to take care of you because of my father. He cared deeply for you Nanny, almost better than he cared for my mother. You want to know why I sent your boy away?"

Nanny nods her head.

"He was trying to do the same thing Aggie is trying to do, recruit slaves to run away. This is my plantation. Any other plantation owner would've hung him from a tree. But no, because my father made me promise not to hurt you or yours, I had to find another way to punish him. Now Aggie is following in his footsteps. I can't have all this disruption on my plantation. This is also the second time this gal has disrespected me and in front of other slaves. If I lose the respect of my slaves, sooner or later, they will all try my patience. I've tried real hard to keep my promise to my father Nanny, but I have no choice now. Aggie will be sold at auction today and you have to leave too."

"Will I go where my Dad is?"

"Maybe, maybe not. All depends on the highest bid. The money is all I care about."

"Massuh Waters, I have nowhere to go," says Nanny.

"I'm sorry Nanny. I've done all I could by you. I'll take you into town when I take Aggie to the auction block. Maybe you can find work there. Honestly, I don't care anymore. I'm done with this obligation."

"What about my mom?" I ask.

"What about her? I have a lot of years of labor left in that wench. She stays."

"So Massuh, you breakin' me way from all my family?" ask Nanny.

"Would you rather I hang Aggie from a tree? You know Rainer will do it. All I have to do is say the word. I've always been kind to you Nanny and took good care of you haven't I?"

"Yes Massuh. I's always took good care of you too."

"Well, the difference here is I'm in charge and I make the rules. You two get your things together. Come sunrise, we're heading into town."

"Please Massuh Waters, I's even go work da fields fo' ya. Let me stay." Mr. Waters ignores Nanny and goes to the door.

"Rainer, I'll be heading to town in about an hour or so. Selling the gal. Have those boys get my carriage ready for travel."

"Yes sir." Mr. Waters brushes past us, returning to his bedroom upstairs.

"Massuh Waters, please!" Nanny continues to plead.

"Nanny, stop it! You are free! Come on." We make our way back to the slave quarters. By now, Maureen and Emy are dressed and have started chores except now Maureen is in the kitchen cooking. Who gave her Nanny's job already? How did they know? Then it dawned on me. Emy snitched on me. She must've gone through my bag while I was asleep since she 'barely slept at night'. I should've known she couldn't be trusted. Maureen must've had her eyes on Nanny's spot so her lovely daughter made a way for it to happen. Move me and Nanny out the way and they just slid on in.

I wash up and get dressed, packing the few things I have in my burlap sack. Nanny is crying while she packs her stuff, all forty-four years' worth (that's how long she's been on this plantation).

"Nanny, it's going to be OK. Please stop crying." I may as well be talking to myself. Then it hits me like a ton of bricks. I have no idea where I'll end up. At least here, I have my mom and Nanny. When I'm sold, I could end up anywhere, with no one to look after me. My chest tightens.

"I have to go and see my mom. I have to say goodbye," I cry.

"Aggie, don't you do nothin' stupid, ya hea?" Nanny yells but I'm halfway across the yard by now. I run so fast, the tears are moving sideways to my ears. I have to get to Mom. If this is it, I might never see her again. I run down the gravel, through the tall field of grass, the same grass I encountered my first day here. Mom is in the fields and I have to get to her to say goodbye. Tears continue to flow. When I get to the edge of the field where the slaves are, I slow down to catch my breath. All of a sudden, someone knocks me to the ground and pulls me from behind. With a hand over my mouth, I'm not able to scream, but I know from the smell who it is. He smells just like the horses in the barn. When Mr. Rainer has me near the creek, I look around and remember picking blackberries with Lettie. Everything seems to be moving in slow motion, even the way Mr. Rainer is pulling at my dress. He stuffs a dirty handkerchief in my mouth to muffle my screams. My squeals sound like the pigs in the barn. Unable to scream for help, I look up in the sky then close my eyes.

Chapter 16

"Doctor, how serious is her concussion? I'm getting nervous because she's been out for a while."

"We're monitoring her brain activity and everything appears to be normal. The CT scan showed no signs of trauma. Temporary memory loss is common in situations such as these, but we won't know until she wakes up. I'll be back to check on her in a little while."

For a minute, I think I'm hallucinating.

"Thanks doctor." That sounds like my dad. I hear a door close and a constant beeping noise. Am I dreaming? I can't be dreaming. I open my eyes. Bright lights cause me to squint. Everything is sterile and bright in here. Where am I? I swear I heard my dad's voice.

"Aggie bear?" There it is again. I try to turn my head but there's a brace on my neck, restricting me from moving. I move my eyes left to right.

"Dad?"

"Yes, I'm here Aggie bear. I'm here." Dad's face comes into view. It's really him.

"Dad?" I can't control the tears.

"What's wrong Aggie? I'm here baby girl, I'm here."

"Oh my God Daddy?!" He wraps his arms around me tight.

"Shhhh calm down sweetie. You have to keep still so you don't hurt yourself again. You have a terrible head injury and they have a brace on your neck."

"What happened? Where am I?"

"You're in the emergency room. Apparently you were in detention hall and tripped over your back pack and fell. Hit your head so hard you were knocked unconscious. Got a nasty gash back there too. We were so worried about you." I can't believe it. I'm back, back in 2016. My uncontrollable crying concerns Dad. But he has no idea what I've been through over the past five days.

"Aggie bear, why are you so upset? Are you in a lot of pain?"

"Dad, you don't understand. I was a slave, it was so real. I got whipped and they were going to sell me and they sold you and Mr. Rainer killed Oscar and......"

"Aggie, Aggie, shhhhh calm down, calm down sweetie. Breathe. Slowly, just breathe." I take deep breaths and try to calm down. I have to let him know what happened to me.

"Dad, please listen, I was so scared. It was horrible. Every time I went to sleep, I kept waking up on the plantation. Then I was trying to make my own freedom papers, but I got caught. That Emy, she snitched. It was so terrible Dad. You weren't there to protect me. I needed you but they sold you. Oh my God Dad, it was so real," I explain while crying.

"Oh Aggie, you must've had a terrible dream while you were unconscious. Poor thing. Let me call the doctor back in here. Maybe he can give you a sedative to calm you down, help you rest."

"NO! I don't want to rest. I want to go home. Please just take me home. Where's Mom? Where's Nanny?"

"They went to the cafeteria to get some coffee. Let me text your mother."

I've never been more happy than I am at this moment. Even though my head is throbbing, my heart is doing jumping jacks. I'm home, back in 2016. And I'm free.

□

About a dozen pink and purple balloons appear through the door before Mom and Nanny appear. Lexi is behind them holding a chocolate birthday cake. I was wondering what was taking them so long to get back from the cafeteria with their coffee. Now I know.

"Happy Birthday!" They all yell together. Mom hands Dad a gift bag and a Burger King bag she'd been carrying. Chocolate cake, balloons and my favorite - Whopper with cheese, no onion extra mayo – now this has got to be the best birthday ever. Freedom is priceless and I don't know what's in that gift bag, but it can't compare to the joy I feel having my freedom back. Tears start to well up in my eyes. Mom rushes over and hugs me tight.

"What's wrong Aggie?"

"I'm just so happy. You all don't understand what I went through. It was all so real." Mom looks over at Dad and he shakes his head.

"Aggie, your dad told me about your dream. I'm so sorry it upset you so much."

"But it was more than a dream. You guys don't believe me but it's true. All of you were there."

"Did you go to the other side or something?" asks Lexi.

"No, but I went back in time, 200 years to be exact. I was a slave for five days. You were there Lexi, but your name was Lettie."

"Lettie? Ewww," says Lexi.

"Five days? You've only been unconscious since yesterday. You slept through your birthday so we decided to bring the party to you," Dad says.

"You went back to 1816?" Mom says this but she's not convinced.

"Yes, and we were all slaves. It was the worst thing that's ever happened in my life."

"It was just a dream Aggie."

"No Mom, it was more than a dream. Something

happened to me. I was hit with a whip, got a lashing for disrespecting Mr. Waters. Then Mr. Rainer killed Oscar because Oscar stood up for Sylvie, his wife. You worked the fields all day and night, so long that your feet were swollen.”

“That sounds like me now,” Mom says, smiling.

“I’m serious Mom. There is nothing funny about anything that happened to me. It was horrible. Mr. Waters sold Dad to another plantation. Nanny worked in the main house and, oh my God, is Dad’s real daddy white?”

“Aggie!” Dad exclaims.

“You know who your Papa is Aggie,” says Nanny.

“Well, in the dream, Mr. Waters’ father was my grandfather! Me, Nanny and Daddy, they referred to us as mulatto because we were part white. Are we part white?” Mom is staring at me with a look of confusion.

“That bump on the head has rattled you up. I’m sure, somewhere down the line there is probably some white in our bloodline. Just what happened in those days to our ancestors. We can’t change the past,” says Nanny.

“Aggie, we are supposed to be celebrating your birthday. This is a happy time! Stop with all of the depressing talk. I’m so relieved you finally woke up, we all are. And look,” she motions for Dad to hand me the gift bag.

“What is this?”

"Just open it silly." I pull out the abundance of tissue paper and finally reach a box. The box is sleek, all white with an apple logo.

"An IPad mini? Oh my God! I thought…"

"Don't worry about all that. We made it happen," says Dad.

"Your dad made it happen," says Mom. They look at each other with affection and smile.

"Thank you so much Mom and Dad. You didn't have to do this. I want to apologize to you guys about being such a brat when I didn't get the gift I wanted for my birthday. Slaves rarely celebrated birthdays and most of them didn't even know when they were born. I appreciate everything you have ever done for me. Mom, I hope you don't have to work overtime much longer. Dad, I hope you find work soon. Until then, I'll never disrespect your authority or make you feel less than a man. You are the man of the house and I can't live without you here with us. And Nanny, thank you for always having my back. You always keep me straight even when I don't listen sometimes. I will take school more seriously. I will respect my teachers and not disrupt class. There was a time when we would get whipped or worse just for trying to learn how to read. I won't ever take education for granted."

"Wow. Who are you and what have you done with my daughter?" Mom says.

"You guys probably think I'm crazy and this is all because I hit my head. But it was real. I was a slave in

1816. I lived it and I learned from it."

"I'm sorry you went through the emotional trauma you did in your dream Aggie. It sounds so depressing and sad. Let's be glad we were born at a different time," says Mom.

"I am glad I was born at a different time. But I'm also glad I got to witness what 1816 Aggie would've gone through."

The adults have tears in their eyes. Lexi is trying to figure out what Lifetime movie she's in the middle of. I know it's probably hard for her to comprehend. She would never understand.

Nanny ties the balloons to the table situated in the corner of the room before coming over to hug me. She hugs me like the bunny on the card and it makes me smile.